HAZURE

THE GUILD MEMBER WHOSE
A WORTHLESS SKILL IS ACTUALLY
A LEGENDARY ASSASSIN

Kennoji

ILLUSTRATION BY
KWKM

It was an ultramarine-colored
offensive spell that I had
seen countless times. Once,
it annihilated an army of
several thousand.

"...That magic. I feel as
though I've seen it before."

"I knew it.
It's Lina."

A demon man had just been about to attack Rila.
I could have killed him immediately, but...

"If Rila is considered a small fry, then you're less than a bug."

HAZURE SKILL

THE GUILD MEMBER WITH
A WORTHLESS SKILL IS ACTUALLY
A LEGENDARY ASSASSIN

3

Kennoji

ILLUSTRATION BY
KWKM

YEN
ON

New York

Hazure Skill: The Guild Member with a Worthless Skill Is Actually a Legendary Assassin, Vol. 3
Kennoji

Translation by Jan Mitsuko Cash
Cover art by KWKM

HAZURE SKILL "KAGE GA USUI" WO MOTSU GUILD SHOKUIN GA, JITSU WA DENSETSU NO ANSATSUSHA Vol. 3
©Kennoji, KWKM 2019
First published in Japan in 2019 by KADOKAWA CORPORATION, Tokyo.
English translation rights arranged with KADOKAWA CORPORATION, Tokyo through TUTTLE-MORI AGENCY, INC., Tokyo.

English translation © 2022 by Yen Press, LLC

Yen On
150 West 30th Street, 19th Floor
New York, NY 10001

Visit us at yenpress.com
facebook.com/yenpress
twitter.com/yenpress
yenpress.tumblr.com
instagram.com/yenpress

First Yen On Edition: February 2022

Yen On is an imprint of Yen Press, LLC.
The Yen On name and logo are trademarks of Yen Press, LLC.

Library of Congress Cataloging-in-Publication Data
Names: Kennoji, author. | KWKM, illustrator. | Cash, Jan Mitsuko, translator.
Title: Hazure skill, the guild member with a worthless skill is actually a legendary assassin / Kennoji ; illustration by KWKM ; translation by Jan Mitsuko Cash.
Other titles: Hazure sukiru kage ga usui o motsu girudo shokuin ga jitsu wa densetsu no ansatsusha. English
Description: First Yen On edition. | New York : Yen On, 2021.
Identifiers: LCCN 2020055761 | ISBN 9781975318772 (v. 1 ; trade paperback) | ISBN 9781975318796 (v. 2 ; trade paperback) | ISBN 9781975318819 (v. 3 ; trade paperback)
Subjects: LCSH: Assassins—Fiction. | GSAFD: Fantasy.
Classification: LCC PL872.5.K46 H3913 2021 | DDC 895.63/6—dc23
LC record available at https://lccn.loc.gov/2020055761

ISBNs: 978-1-9753-1881-9 (paperback)
        978-1-9753-1882-6 (ebook)

10 9 8 7 6 5 4 3 2 1

LSC-C

Printed in the United States of America

HAZURE SKILL

THE GUILD MEMBER WITH
A WORTHLESS SKILL IS ACTUALLY
A LEGENDARY ASSASSIN

CONTENTS

1
R & R Trip, Part I

"Oh, Mr. Roland, look at this! It's the ocean! The ocean!" Milia exclaimed with her head sticking out of the carriage window.

"Stop that, Milia; it's dangerous."

After our manager, Iris, gave her a warning, Milia let out an embarrassed giggle, then she sat down.

There were six of us in the carriage, Milia, Iris, three other women, and myself. A second conveyance trundled alongside ours filled with men.

"I'm so excited. It's been such a long time since I've been outside Lahti." Milia's eyes glittered as she gazed out the window.

"I suppose we could call this a silver lining. We were lucky enough for the events to convene," Iris remarked.

Yesterday, the Lahti branch where we worked had received a commendation from the guild headquarters.

"Well, Mr. Roland was the actual reason that happened, though," added Milia.

We had been recognized for our quest-processing rate, the success of adventurers from our office, and so on. We'd received a five-hundred-thousand-rin bonus, along with a letter of praise from the guild master.

"It's an achievement—a huge one—for a branch in an insignificant town to receive public recognition from headquarters," Iris commented.

"I'm sure we owe it to everyone's efforts," I replied.

Although she sounded exasperated, Iris smiled. "You really are so modest."

On the same day, a pair of adventurers, more specifically, a man and a woman, had gotten into a lover's quarrel and had caused a magical explosion in the Lahti Adventurers Guild. Luckily, no one had been hurt, and we'd saved all our important documents.

"So the repairs will take a week?"

"Yes. That's why it's all right for us to take this two-night, three-day vacation. The bonus helps as well."

During our absence, the office was closed. The trip wasn't mandatory, but the remittance from guild headquarters was covering all our expenses.

"I shall accompany you...! Unless you wish to spend your time in tedium at our abode, knave!"

When I had explained the situation to Rila, she'd been very excited and had decided to come with me. And just as Rila had said, the only thing I could have done if I'd stayed at home was train myself.

"I see; the maiden becomes excited about something as tawdry as the ocean," Rila whispered from my bag in her black-cat form as she observed Milia shouting about the ocean.

"You practically lost yourself in excitement over the Somaleel coast not too long ago," I responded quietly. Rila immediately pulled a face.

"'Twas...simply surprise that the seas of the mortal world would be so fair."

I shrugged.

The Somaleel coast had a luxury resort often frequented by royalty and thus was fancier than similar places. That said, we hadn't gone there for pleasure. King Randolf had called upon me through the Adventurers Guild. The neighboring Holy Land of Rubens's prince and our own princess, Almelia, had been arranged to be wed, and King Randolf had wanted me there to guard them. He'd likely already been cautious of King Rubens, considering he'd dealt with the man already. I'd noticed some undesirable things myself, and the engagement had been called off after I'd uncovered a sinister plot.

Rila was undoubtedly looking sullen because she'd been so excited over the ocean the first day of that excursion she'd wandered away and gotten lost.

The carriage rolled onward toward our destination.

"I spy only females in this transport," Rila observed. "And they all have high posts as well."

"It must be a coincidence," I replied. "Plus, I do have a title myself as the dedicated proctor for adventurer exams."

"How impressive is that, really?" Rila questioned.

"Enough to get me into a seminar in the capital."

"So you claim it to be a high-status position, then?"

"I went to the capital to attend a seminar for work... I believe that makes it quite standard. I think it fits right into the category of *normal* work."

Rila stared at me, looking very serious.

"Must you act so smug?" she asked.

Ignoring the inquiry, I kept the conversation going. "The port city we're headed to should be very lively. Make sure you don't lose your purse or get pickpocketed this time."

"I know. I will not let the same mishap occur again," Rila assured. I truly hoped so. "Is Dey aware of our trip?"

Dey—Candice Minelad—was a vampire and a former member of the demon lord's army. She'd missed out on returning to Hell and had taken the adventurer exam, which she'd passed. Since she specialized in night jobs and was beautiful to boot, she regularly accepted unique jobs. However, staying out in the sun weakened her, and that vulnerability had resulted in her temporarily becoming involved in a horrific incident. After that ordeal, she had said she wanted me to drink her blood. To vampires, making such a request meant they were giving themselves to that person. I hadn't had a reason to refuse, so I'd obliged.

"Had I run into her, I could have told her. I put up a notice, and I'm sure she'll more or less realize what happened after seeing the office," I responded.

Great as she was at her job, she often received all kinds of challenging quests. I thought this would be a good vacation for Dey as well.

"Have you told that somewhat cacophonous elf that we're going to be out for a few days?" I questioned.

"A somewhat cacophonous elf? Ah, you mean Roje. I have not. Well, I am sure she will manage," answered Rila.

Roje was an elf and former member of the demon lord's army who adored Rila. Occasionally she stopped by our house to find something to criticize me about. It was clear she disapproved of my association with Rila, who had once been called the strongest demon lord of all time.

Milia cocked her head at me. "Mr. Roland, what have you been mumbling about?"

"Oh, sorry, nothing at all."

I pushed Rila back into my bag, earning a yowl from the cat.

"Are you planning on buying anything once we get to Kohtoka, Mr. Roland?"

Our destination, the port town of Kohtoka, was filled with marine products and exotic merchandise imported from foreign provinces.

"No, nothing in particular," I said.

"Really? Since it's so close to the beach, I brought a swimsuit!" Milia pulled the outfit in question out of her bag to show it to me, prompting responses from the others in the carriage.

"Oh, I didn't bring one," a woman admitted.

"It's all right. I'm sure they'll have some for sale over there," Milia assured her.

"A swim *soot*...?" Having pushed her face out of the bag again, Rila tilted her head quizzically. Perhaps Hell lacked natural bodies of water to swim in.

Turning to Iris, Milia inquired, "Have you brought one, Branch Manager?"

"I—I don't need a swimsuit, as far as I'm concerned..."

The other women were grinning at their superior.

◆

Eventually, the carriage arrived at the port, and we came to an inn a ways from the center of town. The ocean was visible from my room's window, giving the place an attractive ambience.

I returned Rila to her original form.

"Excuse me, Mr. Rolaaand? Would you care to join me while I look around town?" Milia poked her head into the room as she called for me. "Oh! Miss Prima Donna...what are you doing here...?! This is a trip just for the employees, you know."

"Do not be so fastidious. Knave, I shall accompany Milia to purchase this swim soot or whatever such contraption that is!" Rila latched on to Milia's arm and tugged her away.

"Wha—? But I wanted Mr. Roland."

"Sorry, Miss Milia. Could you keep an eye on her?" I requested.

"Oh... I suppose I don't have much of a choice."

I was worried about Rila losing her way again, but she would be all right with Milia around. The two departed hand in hand.

Our lodgings didn't provide meals, so we could eat wherever we pleased, according to Iris. I planned on wandering about to find a place soon.

Suddenly, a lackadaisical voice announced, "I'm coming in." Dey then entered my room.

"...What are you doing here?" I asked.

"Since the Lahti office was closed, and I've come to the Kohtoka branch for jobs before, I decided I would work here today. Then I spotted you and the others."

So that was it.

"...Did you find out anything about what happened?" I questioned. Dey was investigating a matter on my behalf.

When we had traveled to the Somaleel coast for Almelia's betrothal meeting, I'd reunited with a former fellow member of the party of heroes, Elvie. After that, she had started sending letters for me to the guild roughly once a month. Most of them inquired about my private life or chronicled recent happenings in her own. One particular thing she had mentioned stuck out to me, so I had asked Dey to look into it.

"My, a human pushing a vampire around," Dey said. "You are something special, Master Roland."

"You are mine, aren't you?" I replied.

"I was only joking." She glided over like a snake and loosely wrapped her arms around me from behind. "It was so easy gathering info from Kohtoka. It seems there has been an increase in humans using the substance you speak of in the pleasure quarter."

"I see."

In one of her letters, Elvie had written about the increased usage of a strange drug that had ill effects on human users. Though it provided a temporary high, it would destroy the body.

"Since Kohtoka sees so much tourism, it's probably easy to bring into Kohtoka," Dey explained. "Dispell might purify them of their condition, but it can't do anything at all about the addiction."

"How troublesome."

"I kept an eye on the brothels for a few days. There was one who looked particularly suspect."

"Could you take me there?" I requested.

There were a lot of people using the drug while unaware of its side effects. At the rate it was spreading, it could even reach Lahti. I couldn't ignore it.

◆

I left the inn with Dey, and we made our way to a section of the pleasure district.

"This establishment only popped up recently," Dey told me. "Apparently, the women there are of higher quality and have been stealing customers from older establishments."

Gaudily dressed women in front of the brothels of the pleasure district enticed the men walking along the streets at dusk. The scarlets, purples, yellows, and pinks of both the buildings and the ladies' clothing assaulted the eye. All the colors were indicative of poison in nature.

Our destination was through a back way, and as we entered one of the alleys, I heard a voice.

"I-is it true? That I could make a hundred thousand rin by working for just one day?"

"Yes, miss, and I'm sure you could fetch an even higher sum. It'd be perfect spending money for your trip."

A young man was leading Milia along.

"Oh my, isn't she from the guild?" Dey asked.

"She was supposed to be with Rila... Did they get separated?"

Clearly, Milia had been enticed by the man's sweet-talking.

"She's very much a sheltered country girl, I see," Dey remarked.

"Milia hasn't seen much beyond her hometown. She's probably never met a swindler before and doesn't know how to deal with it."

"Oh, Master Roland, it's that man. A lot of people have said they've gotten the drug from him."

"I see. I'll ask him some questions. Dey, could you find Rila? I'm sure she's gotten lost."

"Okaaay," Dey replied. "Please make sure to be careful, though."

"Who do you think you're talking to?"

"Ha-ha... Your self-confidence matches your strength... How lovely."

Dey kissed my forehead, then she pulled her hood low over her eyes and took off.

"Miss...Milia, was it? Do you have any experience with anything smutty?"

"Wha—?! Why are you asking me that? I—I don't..."

"In that case, you'll fetch an even greater price!"

I wanted to chide her for getting wrapped up in such a clichéd situation.

"Of course, it's her own fault for letting herself get tricked—" I emerged from the alleyway onto the back road.

There was no need for in-depth conversation with the man. I grabbed his arm and pinned him down in an instant.

"Gah?! Wh-who the hell are you?!"

"M-Mr. Roland…? What are you doing here?"

"Miss Milia, this man will force you to do something immodest if you go with him," I told her.

Milia flushed red. "Whaaat?! H-he never mentioned that…"

"I don't think he would. You might not have been able to get home if you'd followed him."

At that, Milia went quiet. She was an innocent girl who had no experience dealing with anyone but her hometown's safe and kind people. This was possibly her first time interacting with someone dubious.

"Miss Milia, I need to speak to this man. This isn't a place for girls unless they have a specific type of business in mind. I suggest returning to the street you came from."

"O-okay…"

Milia was bewildered, but she turned away and ran to the bustling thoroughfare.

"You thinkin' you can get away with this?! Hunh?!" the man shrieked.

"Don't shout. I would've done the same regardless of who the person was or where they came from."

Dey had said this guy was the one distributing the drug.

Glaring at him, I questioned, "Have you heard of a drug called Second?"

"I've got no idea what you're—"

I bent his pinkie the wrong direction.

Plunk. I felt it softly give way.

"GAAAAAAH!"

"I'll ask you again. If you insist on feigning ignorance, I can break every bone in your body, although that would benefit neither of us. I'd rather not listen to the racket you make with each snap."

"I already told you: I don't know!"

"You have some pep; I'll give you that. Now, how many fractures until you change your tune?"

"Wait. Please, just wait!" the man begged. "A-all I've been told is to nab as many useful women as I can and have them take that whatever-it's-called drug."

I'd touched his pinkie. In actuality, the bone was far from broken. A planted notion could be much stronger than anyone would expect. Just a bit of pain accompanied by a sound was enough to convince someone a bone had snapped.

According to the man, he would take women, sometimes by force, and make them work. Thankfully, he'd treated Milia a little more gently. He would occasionally buy them from slave merchants, but he targeted beautiful women he saw on the streets more regularly. Then they would give the prostitutes Second and have them sell the drug to the clientele.

"I-it's not just me, neither. Three others are doing the same exact thing. We get our stock from the master."

I grabbed the man by the lapels and hauled him up.

"Yeek! What are you—?"

I told him what was going on in a region of the Holy Land of Rubens. "The stuff you're peddling is a poison that rots people from the inside out—both their minds and their bodies. They become addicted to chasing the temporary high, and as they keep using it, they lose their sense of self and forget who they are. The more who indulge while unawares, the more victims there will be. They won't be *normal* anymore. At this rate, your friends, your lovers, even your family will become unable to live without Second."

Shocked, the man mumbled, "…That's…what the drug does…? B-but he's supposed to use the profits to help the town… That's what the master said…"

How gullible could this guy be?

I didn't know how the money was flowing, but there was no way anyone selling a drug like this would use the funds to benefit others.

"Is this 'master' the one who gives you orders? Where is he?" I demanded.

"H-he shows up at the establishment sometimes. I don't really know who the guy is myself… He's got red hair and sharp eyes."

"Tell me everything you know about him."

I lowered the man to his feet and had him walk me to the brothel he'd mentioned.

Apparently, he'd been a criminal until this "master" recently took him in. The promise of easy money had lured the man in.

"The master shows up about twice a week, and he brings the goods whenever he does. No one knows where he gets it from. There are tons of warehouses all around Kohtoka that have been active recently, however. He might be bringing it in from there."

My threats paid off, for the man outlined everything to me. He must have truly believed selling the drug was a good thing. After learning the truth was precisely the opposite, he became willing to cooperate.

"Is this master fellow making the drug then?" I questioned.

"I'm not that far in the know."

Based on what the man was saying, the master used the brothel to transfer his supply of Second.

The services cathouses typically offered were already hush-hush, and anyone partaking in such activities would do so behind closed doors. Thus, a brothel was the perfect place to also quietly engage in *other* indulgences.

The establishment was at the center of the pleasure district.

I could tell on sight that the women pandering to the customers on the street were of a different quality compared to the other places. I had expected them to look listless, but instead, some had vivacity in their eyes. A man was calling out each of the women's prices.

"...That's much cheaper than I expected."

"Y-yeah... The sell is that we have great gals at a lower price than the competition."

It was quite an attractive offer for someone drunk on vacation freedom.

"According to the girls, it feels amazing going at it after taking the drug…so the clients and the girls are all hooked on it," the man said before urging me to follow him to the back of the building.

There I saw a summoning circle in a corner.

"This is……"

When I inspected it more closely, I discovered that it was a Gate. It seemed the characteristic red hair the man had described was that of a demon. The demonic court's criteria were esoteric, but if I recalled correctly, Gate was penta-rank, with mono being the highest form.

Roje hadn't been able to learn Shadow, which was court-order-rank tetra magic. That meant the master equaled or exceeded Roje in ability.

"I don't think the master will be here today, though…," the man admitted.

"No, that's fine. This is enough. If you really care about the town, I recommend destroying all the drugs you have. Got that?"

"Y-yessir…!"

I watched the man head through the back door, then go to inspect the Gate. It was just as I'd surmised. A path linked it.

"Time to find out where this connects to."

I used the Gate to jump so I could trace the master's trail.

The spell placed me on the top of a hill. A large fence stood before me, barring entry to a path toward a mansion. Behind was a winding road that snaked down the slope to the section of town where I'd been moments ago.

Guards stationed nearby leveled their spears at me upon my abrupt appearance.

"H-hey! Who the hell are you?!"

"This is Baron Marty Cuthra's private residence. If you haven't got any business here, then scram!"

A baron... So that's where the fabrication about improving the town had come from.

"I didn't think the feudal lordship would have skin in this," I muttered.

It wouldn't do to have the gatekeepers cause a commotion, so I activated my skill, Unobtrusive. I disappeared from sight immediately.

"Where did he go...?"

I silently climbed the wall right beside the guards, landed inside the complex, then looked at the building and assessed the layout, judging by its shape. Based on experience, the head of the household would be on the top floor and would choose a room with an excellent view.

"...Maybe there?"

I sprinted through the front garden and up a pillar before kicking off it. I grabbed the floor of what seemed to be the second-story entrance and handily pulled myself inside. So long as you knew the physical capabilities of your own body, it wasn't challenging.

Reaching for a nearby drain spout, I tested how much weight it could carry before pulling myself even farther up.

I caught sight of the veranda of the room I was headed toward and spotted a middle-aged man beyond the window.

"Hng?!" When his eyes met mine, he let out a startled cough. The cigar he'd been smoking fell to the floor.

Once I was standing on the balcony, he demanded in a panicked tone, "Wh-who are you?! Th-this is the third floor!"

"I'm a suspicious character."

"Y-you dare mock me! S-someone! Is anyone here?!"

I kicked the glass in and entered.

"Nghhhh?! Wh-who are you?! Do you realize I am Marty Cuthra, you brute?!"

"I don't care who you might be. I'm from the kingdom of Felind's special public welfare division."

"What the hell is that…? I've never heard of such a thing."

That was because I'd just made it up.

"It's not part of a royal organization. You can think of it as a sort of secret service that reports directly to King Randolf himself."

"D-directly to H-His Majesty…?! A secret service?!"

No such thing existed.

"We received word about a strange drug that has become prevalent in this area, and we've launched an investigation. It seems something very similar occurred in Rubens not too long ago. I will be reporting back to His Majesty about this."

"W-w-w-wait! A lord is meant to govern his fiefdom. What I do within my territory is my own business!"

"The land isn't yours. And neither are those living in it. They all belong to the kingdom. The king simply entrusts the safekeeping of the territory to the nobility and allows them to run it... The punishment for allowing Second to spread will not be light."

"Grrr...!" Baron Cuthra ground his teeth and turned red in the face. "The people are meant to provide for the lordship! In this place, I am the law. I am the ruler!"

He grabbed a sword hanging on the wall and drew the weapon from its scabbard, readying himself.

"I suspected as much," I remarked idly. "A pig can only think as far as what will fatten his own stomach."

Baron Cuthra let out a strangled cry as he lunged at me with his blade.

Fwoom! The sword flew by the tip of my nose as I evaded the baron's slash. Then I stepped toward my opponent. As we slipped past each other, I sunk my fist deep into Baron Cuthra's face—a fundamental counterattack.

"Fwgah?!" the corrupt noble exclaimed as he flew back. He did a few somersaults before striking the far wall.

"It would do you well to learn how precious normal lives are," I told him.

I explained everything from start to finish to King Randolf, who'd been ignorant of the recent drug crisis.

"...So this dangerous substance that goes by the name of Second spread from the port town that Baron Cuthra governs, I see."

King Randolf glanced at the culprit in question.

Though Baron Cuthra had made plenty of excuses—and contradictory ones at that—to explain away the events that had transpired, King Randolf hadn't listened. At present, the disgraced noble was hanging his head in shame as he reflected on his crimes.

"According to the letter from Elvie, a region in Rubens is in the same state," I stated.

"I see. So you determined that if anything was going on, it would be happening in a port town."

"Part of my discovering this was a coincidence as well," I admitted.

I couldn't have predicted that the branch office would abruptly receive a bonus that led to a vacation in Kohtoka. Regardless, I had made the right decision asking Dey to conduct an investigation.

"We will immediately designate the drug as hazardous in the kingdom of Felind. Severe punishments will be meted out to those involved in the Second's manufacture, sale, or use. So, Baron Cuthra, it seems you're in for a harsh sentence. We will not make allowances for you."

King Randolf declared that the baron would be stripped of his title, territory, and assets on the spot without exception.

"Spreading that drug to line your own pockets is wicked indeed. What's more, Kohtoka is a place of international commerce. You may have created trouble for other nations as well. I will need to look into the situation before deciding on a punishment. You may relax in a cell until then."

Right as he had been about to call aides to send Baron Cuthra away, I stopped him.

"There's something else I still need to ask him. I'm certain he was the one who popularized Second, however, we don't know who made it. I'm reasonably confident it's a demon."

King Randolf scowled. "A demon, you say...?"

"Yes. I found a Gate, which is transportation magic that humans do not use. Hey, Baron Cuthra. Did that demon make the drug? Or was he merely working from another? Tell us what you know."

Baron Cuthra turned white as a sheet as he repeatedly whispered, "I'm going to be killed..."

◆Rila◆

Three hours before Baron Cuthra had been apprehended, Rila had gone with Milia to the bustling market to pick out a swimsuit.

"So what is a swim soot?" Rila inquired.

"You're trying to buy one without knowing what it is...?" Milia replied, confused. "It'd be difficult to swim while wearing regular clothes, right? So it's kind of like a type of garment that you can get wet."

Rila looked puzzled. "Would it not be acceptable to simply swim in the nude?"

"No. That's lewd and indecent! You wouldn't be able to walk along the beach."

"No one will be able to see if one simply undresses after entering the water."

Milia, looking very serious, took Rila by the shoulders. "That's not the issue. That's not the issue at all."

"Y-you have a most frightening look in your eyes…," Rila remarked.

"Swimsuits give girls the chance to dress cute!"

"Oh… Oh…?"

Though she didn't fully comprehend Milia's meaning, Rila was carried along by the other woman's fervor and nodded.

"When someone I like sees me, I want to be wearing something nice, even if it's store-bought. That's every girl's wish!"

"I-is that so…?" Rila truly *didn't* understand, but Milia was so passionate that Rila gave the human a vague nod. Regardless, she was soon spellbound by various articles of clothing lining the shop counters.

"Oh, this swimsuit is cute!" Milia exclaimed. "I wonder… What would you look good in, Miss Prima Donna?"

With narrowed eyes, Milia scanned Rila from her feet to her bust.

"Ha-ha! There is no such thing as a garment that does not suit me. Come now, you may choose my attire," Rila declared.

Frowning, Milia replied, "I wish I had your self-confidence *and* your looks…" Milia entered a shop and began assessing the establishment's merchandise. "I wonder which one would look best?"

Then there was a development…

Rila turned around, feeling as though she'd caught a glimpse of a face she recognized in the bustling marketplace.

Short red hair. The muscles of that neck, the shape of the back.

"It is him..."

The former demon lord left Milia behind and wove through the crowd, disappearing into the throng.

There was something different and not quite humanlike about the red-haired man—something that only another demon could sense. That was what urged Rila to pursue him.

Rila hoped she'd been mistaken, that it wasn't who she thought. Still, if she was correct, and he was struggling to get by in this world, she hoped to send him home to Hell.

With his abilities, he could have gone home on his own. However, Rila suspected he may have lost the power to return.

Her own compassion for her former subordinates and her guilt for being on the losing side of the war pushed her legs along.

"P-please wait."

The crowd kept Rila from reaching the red-haired man, and although she called to him, there was no sign he heard her.

Unwilling to lose sight of the red-haired man, Rila gave chase as he grew more distant. He headed farther away from town until they arrived in an industrial section with many large warehouses. The place was nearly deserted, and Rila was confident he would hear her now. She wanted to see his face.

"Luther... Luther, is that you...?"

The man unlocked a small door and headed into one of the

warehouses. As he did so, Rila caught sight of his profile. There could be no mistaking him now.

Rila had been told Luther had perished in battle, but that report had evidently been mistaken. Tears formed in the corners of Rila's eyes, and her throat grew tight.

"...Luther."

She tried to enter the same way he had, but it was locked. Instead, she peeked into a nearby window to see what he was doing in such a place. Several full sacks were piled up.

"What is that...? I cannot see Luther."

A shadow slipped over Rila from behind, and she felt someone seize her shoulders.

"Lord Rileyla."

"...Oh, it is only you, Dey. Whatever are you doing in a place like this?"

"Master Roland asked me to look for you. Shall we head home?"

"Dey, please listen. It is Luther. Luther is alive. He went into this warehouse just moments ago."

"His Highness is here...?" Gloom crossed Dey's beautiful face. "You're sure it's not someone else? ...I suppose it must be him if you're the one saying so."

Dey looked through the same pane that Rila had. "Huh? Those bags... Oh dear, oh dear. This is a disaster. I need to let Master Roland know. If His Highness is involved in this, I won't be able to help much when push comes to shove, sunset or not..."

"Hmm? Dey, do you know what those sacks are?"

"Yes. Please listen carefully, Lord Rileyla. That is—"

The pair heard footsteps and turned around. A red-haired man stood before the two women, with the glow of the setting sun at his back.

"I thought I heard someone out here, but to think it was my very own sibling and Candice... I had thought you dead, Sister. Nay, I daresay I sense no mana coming from you... Are you truly my sister?"

"Luther, I am so glad you are alive! As you can see, I am in good health. Though, due to certain circumstances, I have lost my mana."

Dey stood in front of Rila, as though to protect her.

"Your Highness...what are you doing in such a place?" the vampire questioned.

"What is it to you?" Luther replied. "Leave."

"Tsk..." Dey clicked her tongue at the command. Roland's aura was like keen lightning, but Luther's was more heavy and oppressive.

"Luther, let us return to Hell," Rila offered. "Roje ventures between here and home from time to time. You may join her."

"Why would I go back to that place? Don't order me around. I much prefer things here. No one compares me to any prodigies, and I can be myself. The food is good, and there are plenty of beautiful women."

Dey grabbed Rila's arm just as the former demon lord was about to say something. The vampire shook her head.

"…Let's go home, Lord Rileyla."

"B-but…"

Rila tried to say more to Luther, but Dey pulled her back. A cold sweat formed on Dey's nape as she led the other woman away, steadily picking up the pace.

"Wait, Candice. What do you know?"

"No…nothing… Not me…"

Luther ranked even higher than a division commander. In the former demon lord's army, Luther had been a corps commander. He was also Rila's younger brother. While nowhere near his sibling's prodigious level, he was much more powerful than Dey.

Rila turned a pleading look to her brother, imploring him to explain.

"…Sister, or shall I say Demon Lord, I thought you had perished."

"I am very much alive," Rila answered.

"There is no such thing as a demon lord without mana. In which case, you must be an impostor, an insolent charlatan who has dared to take on the name Demon Lord. The punishment for tarnishing my elder sister's name shall be death."

Luther's words didn't make sense to Rila. Dey pushed the confused woman by the shoulders.

"Run, Lord Rileyla. He was famous within the army for *hating* his sibling, for despising *you*. Now that you can't fight back, he has the perfect chance to kill you."

Dey summoned her bloodsucking spear and held it in her hands. The crimson colors of dusk filled the sky.

"Hmph. You want to fight? Fine," Luther stated. "This will be the first time I've had fun like this in a while!"

A bellicose smile flitted across Luther's face as he coated his arms in mana. He was using an advanced technique called Magi Raegas.

The usual smile on Dey's face vanished.

"Please stop, both of you!" Rila shouted. "I do not understand the meaning of any of this!"

"His Highness is spreading a highly addictive drug that has nasty effects on humans. Master Roland asked me to look into it."

"What...? A harmful drug? Luther, is this true?"

"I don't have to answer that."

The moment Luther moved, Dey maneuvered her spear and thrust it forward with precision. However, the conclusion of the fight came swiftly. Luther plunged his left arm through Dey's chest, splattering the woman's blood.

"Aghhhah..."

"Hmph. You're nothing."

Luther kicked Dey away. The bloodsucking spear clattered to the ground and disappeared as its master collapsed. Vampire or no, that was a fatal wound. Luther's strike had pierced her chest.

Watching, Rila pleaded with her friend, even knowing that it was a worthless gesture. "Dey? Come on... Dey!"

She shook the other woman's convulsing body, but Dey was silent.

Luther lorded over the two. "It must be fate for us to have met here... No, I suppose it's destiny. I have always hated you, Sister.

You, a prodigy?! The strongest demon lord in history?! I do not know what has transpired, but I see the mess that has come of it! You're nothing but a small fry! Disappear!"

This was a grudge the man had undoubtedly been carrying for years.

His face contorted with murderous joy, and he raised his bloodstained arm over his sibling. And as he did, something like a shadow sidled up next to Luther.

To Rila's eyes, it seemed no more than a fleeting shape, but she knew it to be Roland.

Accompanied by a terrific sound, Roland's fist made direct contact with Luther. Rila heard a crunch as her savior appeared in full view.

Luther went flying, crashing loudly into a warehouse's wall and breaking through.

"If Rila is considered a small fry, then you're less than a bug."

◆Roland◆

According to Baron Cuthra, the master always "disappeared" from within the estate.

He was very likely using a Gate to travel.

I had found such a spell in the corner of a hallway and jumped to follow after him. That led me to a street of warehouses on the outskirts of the town.

That was when I witnessed him in the middle of the crime—the demon man had been moments from attacking Rila.

I could have killed him immediately, but I needed to question him about Second. The demon recovered from my punch and stood in the hole in the wall.

"I was wondering who could have interrupted, but you're just a human."

"That's my younger brother, Luther Diakitep," Rila explained to me.

"He was a corps commander... Dey never stood stand a chance against him." I glanced at the vampire. Anyone could tell it was too late for her. As Luther slowly approached, I told him, "I was planning on capturing you and bringing you with me, but I've changed my mind."

Luther shot me a sarcastic smile. "Have you, now? And what does a mere human hope to achieve against me?"

"I can kill you," I stated.

I could feel Rila's eyes on me for a moment, but she stopped soon enough.

"A lowly being like you?"

"That's right. You're nothing more than an insect."

My rage had me seeing red, so I took a deep breath. That cleared away the anger and calmed me down. "I would like you to tell me something before you go. What is Second? Did you make it?"

"There's no use explaining things to a dead man," Luther answered.

"I see. That's too bad."

The drug had to be stored somewhere nearby. I intended to turn some of it over to King Randolf. It would take some time, but he would find out what it was through analysis.

Luther shrouded his arms in mana. That must have been what he'd used against Dey. I remembered that Rila had called it Magi Raegas.

I activated Unobtrusive and immediately moved into Luther's blind spot.

"Where did—?"

He had fully lost sight of me.

"You seem to have mastered an advanced technique," I commented.

"Huh?!" Luther whirled around, facing me again. "Guh! Did you use some manner of spell?!"

"That's going overboard," I replied. "It's simply a loser skill."

Luther hurled a jab from his left, but I evaded handily.

The demon threw multiple punches at me, and I could hear them whistling past my ears. The air smelled as though it were burning.

"...That's not nearly enough, not even close. You lack experience, skill, thought, finesse, and most of all strength. You've never fought against anyone more powerful than yourself, have you?"

Luther was a sheltered prince who had risen via talent alone.

"Arrrrrrrghhhh!"

Again the demon lashed out at me, but I still had enough time to offer my idle thoughts.

"The demon lord didn't give me time to think. Yet with you, I can speak quite plainly. That's only because I don't need to concentrate on the battle at hand. And despite that, you think you're a match for me?"

If Luther continued to attack wildly, he'd exhaust himself. He'd underestimated me.

"Balancing your offense and defense is vital to surviving in hand-to-hand combat. Didn't your mother teach you that?"

I aimed for an opening, seizing Luther by the head with one hand and tossing him to the ground.

"Ghhk?!"

"You've dedicated yourself entirely to striking as though your victory is assured... But even I can cast that spell."

To demonstrate, I shrouded my right hand with mana. From his spot in the dirt, Luther's eyes widened.

"But...?! Magi Raegas requires delicate mana control...! A human such as you could never—"

"It seems you pride yourself on this technique, but it's nothing all that spectacular. Humans aren't as incapable as you believe."

Rila chose that moment to speak up. "Luther... You should never have fought against him. He is the very man who defeated me and sealed my mana with this collar."

"Why are you siding with him?! This must be a joke! Where is your demon pride?!"

I slapped Luther across the face. "Don't talk about pride. At least know when to be embarrassed. Rila is trying to save you. She hopes to find all her subordinates who were displaced after the war and get them home. That's how deep her compassion for her people is."

"Tch." Luther gritted his teeth.

"It is true. I may not know shame... However, I love this man."

"I knew it! You weren't meant to be the demon lord! You don't have what it takes! I... I am the one who should hold that title...!"

"And does becoming the demon lord involve acting as a drug dealer in the human world? If so, then the position seems far less appealing than it sounds," I quipped.

"Luther, whether demon or human, it does not matter," Rila said. "Cast aside any presumptions that one is superior."

"How dare you say such a thing! Do you realize how many of my comrades followed your order, and...!! Not another word! If you are evil, you must stick to it! There should never be compassion on your face! The demon lord is supposed to—"

"Yes, I wholeheartedly agree," Rila cut in. "That is what the demon lord ought to be. Because my magic was labeled as supreme, many high-ranking militarists held me as a shining example. However, I never concerned myself with which species was best. I evaded such discussions. Regrettably, there was a limit to how long I could keep that up. Had we continued in such a manner, demon society would have split between those who supported the demon lord and those who supported the militarists. The war was a political decision." After a tired sigh, Rila continued, "It is also the demon lord's duty to carry burdens. And that includes taking the blame."

It was an unexpected line of reasoning for the strongest, most fiendish demon lord there was. Luther, who seemed to be hearing this for the first time as well, went silent. The fervor he'd displayed earlier was gone. His mental image of the demon lord and the Rila before him were undoubtedly at complete odds.

"I strove to be the perfect demon lord you describe, Luther... But I loathed it. It is the reason I hung up my mantle as ruler. This man gave me that opportunity."

Rila closed her eyes and nodded firmly.

Luther, however, was looking at me. "What is going on here...? Damn it... You defeated a prodigy, and you've warped her entire personality... Just how powerful are you? It's disappointing..."

"You're right."

Rila's brother had probably always been in her shadow, not unlike how I'd been lingering in Almelia's. The difference between us was that I'd made an effort to break away.

I plunged my left arm into Luther's chest.

"It seems we both took on disappointing roles," I stated.

My eyes remained trained on Luther's own until he died. It took about two seconds. He didn't suffer much.

"Rila, demons know necromancy, right? Teach it to me."

"There are such types of spells... However, they are forbidden," she replied, not bothering to ask what I intended to do with the magic.

"I don't know the rules of Hell. And we're in the human world," I argued.

"They are banned because of the strain they place on the

caster. The magic transfers part of the caster's life force... Do you understand? In terms of level, it is indisputably within court-order-rank mono."

"I don't care how challenging the theory behind it is. I want to bring Dey back to life."

And so Rila taught me the fundamentals of necromancy, including the summoning circle and processes required for it.

"I cannot even imagine the terrors that would await should you fail... I have only attempted to use it once when I was young. I was successful, yet if the worst should come to pass, you may die."

There was concern in Rila's eyes as she looked up at me.

"I can't let Dey stay like this. I don't mind a little danger."

Together, we drew summoning circles and placed Dey in one. I entered the other and invoked the spell.

A blinding light overtook my vision, and I felt everything around me go black.

When I woke, I saw the ceiling of my room at the inn.

"So I survived."

My body felt all but fused to the bed for how heavy it was. Even raising a single finger seemed like too much.

"That's my line," came a voice. Dey suddenly popped into my vision. She was peering straight down at me.

"...I guess this means it worked," I remarked.

"Lord Rileyla told me what happened. You're so naughty." She gave me a tap on the nose, then pouted angrily. "You learned necromancy to save me, *and* you were even successful… You're so capable."

When it came to human magic, I was stuck within the intermediate range. Perhaps demonic spells suited me better.

"…You had no idea what a mistake might cost you… Why would you do something so asinine…?"

"You're mine, aren't you?" I said. "What I do with your life is my choice."

"Really? Your first instinct is to act suave…?"

Dey planted a kiss on my cheek. It felt nice and cool.

"Do your wounds…hurt?" I asked.

Dey shook her head. "My senses are duller than before. I can't feel when things are hot or cold, either. I'm holding you responsible for this, you know?" Dey slipped into my bed. "Hee-hee. You're helpless right now, aren't you, Master Roland?"

"Looks like the necromancy worked then," I commented.

Dey nibbled on me. "It really has. Now I'm a vampire *and* an undead."

An immortal vampire turning into one of the undead seemed like a huge contradiction. According to Dey, she no longer felt an urge to drink blood. Since the bloodsucking spear was a type of summoning magic, she could still use it, thankfully. From what I could tell, she leaned more on the undead side physically. Otherwise, her abilities were about the same as before.

"You can go outside during daylight now. That seems convenient," I remarked.

"That's not the point. If we fool around now, it's basically necrophilia," Dey responded.

"You can imagine that's not one of my proclivities."

"It's okay. I'll make it good; you'll see. But not right now. I have a giant hole through my chest."

"Want me to fill that opening with hopes and dreams?"

"Oh, Master Roland, really? But the more holes, the better, no?"

Smooch, smooch, nibble, nibble.

I let Dey kiss me and bite me.

Rumble, rumble.

Suddenly, I heard a strange noise and spotted Rila standing in the doorway, her fists trembling.

"I thought I heard voices, so I rushed back... And this is what I find...!"

Dey audibly swallowed and quietly left my bed. "Ah, I suddenly remembered there's something I need to take care of."

Since Rila was blocking the exit, Dey left through the window.

"Really, now. Must I constantly be on guard?" Rila said with dismay.

"How long was I asleep?" I asked.

"A full day. We knew you were successful, but there was no telling how severe the recoil was. Based on your state, it seems minor."

Rila smoothed out my hair from the side of the bed. Her eyes started to fill with tears.

"I was so worried..."

"I'm sorry."

She sniffled. I'd never in my life been so frustrated I couldn't move my own hands.

Rila and Dey had told the other guild staffers I was bedridden with a cold.

"I kissed you so often while you were asleep."

"Really?"

"However, you did not react at all. I was so forlorn."

"Were you?"

"I hoped it would wake you."

"That's too bad it didn't."

Rila slowly brought her tearstained face close to mine. I softly closed my eyes.

"Wait, Branch Manager, I think you should go in later. You'll be a bother to him if you're too pushy."

"I could say the same to you."

When she heard those voices, Rila flung herself away and straightened herself back up. *"Ahem."* She coughed, her face red.

"Miss Prima Donna, how is Mr. Roland doing?"

Milia and Iris were peeking into my room.

"Mm-hmm. As you can see, he has just woken."

"Oh, good." Iris smiled. "We can stay here until tomorrow afternoon, so please take it easy. You still have days off, and you'll need to cover the cost of your room after that, but you can remain here if you like."

"Understood," I answered.

"You must be awfully tired, Miss Prima Donna. Would you like me to take care of him for you?" offered Milia.

"I am fine. You are on a trip. You should do well to enjoy the sea and the beaches."

"B-but…"

Iris tugged on the back of Milia's collar.

"Read the room," she chided.

"Ugh, okay… But Mr. Roland and the ocean…," Milia whined.

"Have some self-control."

"You went all out searching for the right bathing suit, too, didn't you, Branch Manager? Aren't you disappointed?"

"Y you saw that?"

Iris flushed while Milia started to reenact the scene of Iris shopping.

"Now, this one is amaaazing. Oh, the men at the beach will be drooling over this amaaazing—"

Iris pulled Milia out of the room and slammed the door closed behind them.

"I—I did put a lot of thought into it… B-but did I overdo it…?"

"Uh… I-it looked really good…on you…?"

"What kind of reaction was that?… I'm going to buy myself a new one…"

Their banter grew more and more distant.

Rila chuckled to herself.

I only now realized that my bed was surrounded by fruits and flowers.

"It is from all the guild staff," Rila explained to me.

"Seems I've caused them a lot of worry."

"Every single one of them claimed you help them on a regular basis. You were dearly missed, knave."

Was I? I thought while staring absentmindedly at the ceiling. Somewhere along the way, I drifted off to sleep.

◆

Meanwhile, back at the house...

"Lord Rileylaaa! I, Roje Sandsong, have brought your favorite berries from Hell! Human, I have not brought any for you! Th-though, I suppose if you *insist*, I will begrudgingly grant you some... A-anyway, I won't withhold them from you entirely!"

Her loud call was met with only silence from inside the building.

"?"

Upon receiving no answer, Roje let herself in.

"H-huh... No one is here..."

Although feeling a bit lonely, Roje elected to wait for Rila and Roland to return. Surely they wouldn't be away for very long.

However...

"Why...? Why are they not back? It's been days..."

Puzzled, Roje tilted her head.

"Where did the two of them go? Th-they couldn't have... eloped, could they...?! Th-there's no way. Lord Rileyla would never, not with a male human." Roje scowled. "Or perhaps Lord Rileyla is in danger?! …I feel like she might be. I sensed something. Just now. It's my sixth sense."

Presently, a full day had passed since Roland saved Rila from Luther.

"Lord Rileyla…! I, Roje Sandsong, shall guard you with my life! This shall be the symbol of my devotion!"

Roje stood and left the house, heading into town to search for clues.

2
R & R Trip, Part II

We spent another two days at the inn. That was how long it took until I could move my limbs again.

According to Iris, while I was bedridden, the Order of Chivalry had come to the warehouses for inspection. Suspicious articles had been confiscated.

"I feel heavy."

Since I had spent so much time asleep, listlessness gripped every fiber of my being.

"There is no remedy for that. You used court-order-rank mono necromancy to bring a vampire back from the dead. Such exhaustion is an expected result."

"You said you used it once yourself. Who was it for?" I inquired.

"Oretenberg..."

"Who is that?" I pressed.

"'Twas from my past...when I had a pet—a pet cat... It worked well enough, but I was unconscious for several hours. I realized then that the recoil depended upon the target of the spell based on the workings of the summoning circle."

I understood why Rila had been worried about the danger when I'd brought back Dey. There was a big difference between a cat and a vampire.

"I'm not sure whether he made it or brought it here, but I do wonder what that Second stuff that Luther was trying to spread was. Perhaps someone else created it for him...," I pondered aloud. Despite racking my brains while in bed, I hadn't been able to come up with a clear answer.

"Oh yes... It is a type of painkiller used in Hell a generation past. Though, it is not in much use now," answered Rila.

"So he didn't make it, then."

According to her, it shouldn't have possessed a secondary effect. However, the substance was meant for demons. Perhaps Second reacted differently with human bodies. Even Rila couldn't be certain.

"Are your pain medications not drinkable like recovery potions?" I asked.

"You are quite knowledgeable. They are these days. We are able to make liquid analgesics using another variety of herb. That white powder is a more traditional curative. But it was difficult to administer on the battlefield, you see. I imagine a hefty amount of it has gone unused."

Luther must have discovered the substance's adverse effects on humans, but there was no way of knowing how it all started—not anymore.

"He was such a fool," Rila spat with disdain.

Once I had time, I would need to explain everything to King Randolph.

"Oh, Master Roland? Can you move around now?" Dey inquired, making a sudden entrance.

"Yes. I can't fight like usual, but it won't impede my everyday life."

"Hee-hee, I think you're still more than powerful enough, even weakened as you are. You should be fine."

My body's reactions were slower than usual. If I was to liken it to anything, it felt as though something was wrapped around me.

"Well, shall we go, then?" Dey suggested.

"Hmm? Where?" I questioned.

"'Where?'" Dey repeated. "Lord Rileyla, didn't you tell him?"

"Um... I lacked a good opportunity to..."

"Really? You're so bashful about the strangest things."

I wasn't following, so Dey explained things to me, saying, "We're going to the beach. Everyone fiiinally got their act together and picked out swimsuits, so we wanted to go as soon as you could move again..."

Dey glanced at Rila. She was fidgeting bashfully.

"I have qualms about wearing that scrap of cloth... Why can I not go in the nude...?"

That line of reasoning was not one I could follow.

"Just think of it as equipment for the occasion, Lord Rileyla," Dey assured. "It's what's used when underwater. Understand?"

"...Mm-hmm... I see..."

Evidently, the two had already picked out something for me. Dey handed me a pair of swim trunks.

We're going to the ocean, then? I suppose it's as good a time as any.

Nodding, I said, "All right. I'll change and head over."

"Well then, see you later," Dey replied.

After she blew me a kiss, she grabbed Rila, who still looked embarrassed, and they both left the room.

I caught glimpses of people on the beach from my window. One of them noticed me and gave me a big wave.

"Mr. Rolaaand!" they called.

"Is that you, Milia?" I answered.

She wore a skirted swimsuit. I spotted Iris beside her.

"Don't shout," she scolded Milia.

The branch manager glanced at me. She was sporting a straw hat, sunglasses, and a navy bikini. Unlike Milia's attire, hers seemed more adult. I'd been told everyone had a swimsuit, so I supposed Dey and Rila would be wearing them, too.

Rila aside, could Dey actually wear one?

She had the hole through her chest, after all. She would probably fill it with something—maybe an apple or the like.

I changed quickly and headed to the beach.

When Milia spotted me, she ran right over.

"Mr. Roland, I'm so glad to see you're better."

"I'm sorry for worrying you," I replied.

"Well, I personally thought you would be just fine," Iris stated from under a large parasol.

"You were anxious, too, Branch Manager!" Milia said.

"That's enough. If you stay out there, you'll get a sunburn."

"I think you might be the only one worried about that, Branch Manager."

"Fine. Bask in the sun. You'll regret it in a decade."

"I think it's only a matter of course that anyone would get a sunburn going to the beach…"

While they argued over skin issues and such, I started my preparatory exercises.

"…Um, Mr. Roland, what are you doing?" Milia questioned.

"Oh yes, I was thinking of swimming to that island," I told her. I pointed ahead into the ocean.

"Which one…? What?! But that's so small! It's so far! Why would you do that?! We came all this way to enjoy the ocean, though."

"I'm swimming there *because* I've come to the ocean, of course," I explained, not sure why Milia was against the idea. "Swimming makes use of the entire body."

"Uh. Uh-huh…"

"It's the perfect exercise—and very suitable for bringing me back to form after being out of commission," I told her.

"Please don't be so practical." Milia sighed, seemingly having come to a realization. Then she pointed at me. "…When you're at the beach with girls, you enjoy it with them. That's *normal*. Going all out swimming isn't normal, all right?"

"Then let's enjoy ourselves," I decided.

"Yay," Milia replied as she hopped slightly. "Let's make a sandcastle together. Okay?"

"If it's a stronghold you want, I'll have to give some input," I replied.

"That's fine! We'll make it together, so we can discuss it as we go!"

"So we'll assume the enemy, the demon lord's army, is ten thousand strong, and we have five hundred. Let's construct a bastion that will last three months under those assumptions. In which case, we'll need to have a structure to act as a base for the front line that we're prepared to forfeit."

"Think of something fancier, please! You're slaughtering the fun!"

"Yes," I continued. "I think any fortification would do well to envision that the worst could come to pass. Not everything ends peacefully. We should expect some violence."

"I want to make a castle three seconds before the prince and princess fall in love," Milia insisted.

Iris was chuckling from under the parasol.

"All right. Leave the defenses entirely to me, in that case. The prince and princess won't be able to fall in love if they can't defend their home, after all."

"...Ugh... Okay, now you've gone and said something that kind of sounds suave..."

"The prince and princess are prepared to fight when the time comes, so the royal family doesn't have an underground escape route. If the troops were to learn one existed, it would affect morale. We'll say in this premise that they'll either need to protect the castle until reinforcements arrive or face total annihilation."

"You're ruining the fun again!"

"You're right. It would be best if the reinforcements came as soon as possible to avoid the slaughter."

Milia frowned. "Why do you look like you're reliving something from your past? We're just making a sandcastle here."

I had been immersed in constructing the frontline base when a wave rushed in and destroyed just about half of it.

"It seems we've suffered a literal wave assault. Thinking about it another way, that's basically a declaration that having a base here would be bothersome. Heh, all right then..."

"You really seem to be enjoying yourself, Mr. Roland," Milia remarked.

I quickly dug a hole and was erecting a wall as Dey and Rila approached.

"Oh my, Master Roland, are you playing in the sand?"

Dey's bathing suit was much skimpier than the other women's.

"Dey, what about your hole?" I asked, to which Dey scrunched in her shoulders.

She pushed out her ample breasts and forced them to create a valley.

"Hee-hee. When I squish my boobs together, you can't see it, see?"

"I suppose that's true," I replied.

"I'm hiding it on my back with my hair."

Even when she wasn't pushing her chest together, it was already large enough that it concealed the opening well.

Rila wore a T-shirt over her swimsuit.

"Miss Prima Donna, aren't you going to take that off?" Milia questioned.

"Hmm... I simply do not feel at home in this..."

"But you're usually so self-assured," commented Milia.

"This is far more embarrassing..."

"Mr. Roland is staring at you."

"...Rila, whatever you're hiding is going to bother me."

"Ugh..."

As Rila acted bashful, Dey snuck up behind her and caught her arms in a lock. Milia stretched out her hands, itching to pull off the shirt.

"St-stop... I am embarrassed..."

"You're so cute like this, Miss Prima Donna... Now, please stop struggling." Milia laughed ominously as she pulled off the shirt. Rila was wearing a red bikini decorated here and there with ribbons.

"Uh."

"Lord Rileyla, it looks great on you."

"I'm glad I helped you pick it out! ♪"

Dey and Milia nodded to themselves.

Face scarlet, Rila sat curled up on the sand. Her skin was pure white, her shoulders looked delicate, and her navel appeared slender. The cords at her hips were also tied into ribbons. I caught a glimpse of her pale neck under her tied-up hair. I had previously only ever seen her exposed in dim light. Under the bright sun, Rila's skin seemed even more pale and lovely.

"How beautiful," I said.

Rila's face turned an even darker shade of red.

"Y-you fool!"

She threw sand at me, snatched the shirt back from Milia, and ran across the beach, grains crunching under her feet as she went until she came to a stop to hide behind Iris. She was like a stray cat that hadn't yet become familiar with humans.

"I think I'll only spend my time with other people wearing bathing suits," Dey stated.

"You have the right idea," agreed Milia. "Let's do exactly that."

The two of them glanced at Rila, who pulled a face before slowly venturing from the safety of the parasol. Cautiously, she inched forward, resembling a stray kitten still wary after being lured out by food.

"I do not understand why I must wear such a disgraceful outfit... If I must, I would rather strip right here, and—"

"Rila," Milia cut in, "it's a lot more disgraceful to be naked."

Ultimately, Rila lost out to her desire to spend time with the others, and she joined us, exposed skin and all.

First, we played in the sand, then we held a volleyball game, enjoyed some long-distance swimming (no one else joined me), and buried someone in the sand.

Our day at the beach turned out to be far more enjoyable than I'd first surmised. Partway through, an elf made a scene some distance away, but it looked like things quieted down after a bit, and she wandered off somewhere.

As Rila watched the elf being taken away on a stretcher from afar, she muttered, "Wasn't that Roje...?"

It *did* resemble Roje.

"...Does she usually swim in from the ocean?" I asked.

"She typically comes from Hell. So...I suppose it is a different elf."

After that, we enjoyed a barbecue that Iris prepared and had our fill of the beach. Around evening, we headed back to the inn. Upon returning, Rila stood by the mirror and happily checked herself out.

"Hmm. ♪♪♪"

She'd been so reluctant to wear her bikini, yet now she wouldn't take it off for some reason.

◆

While I was eating breakfast in my room the next day, Milia snuck in.

"Mr. Roland, do you have some free time?"

"I do. Since we're heading home tomorrow."

"Y-you're not planning to go out with Miss Prima Donna today, then...?"

"We've got nothing in particular lined up. Rila said she would be looking around the market."

Milia grinned and turned her back to me.

"Yes! Showing Miss Prima Donna all those things she'd want paid off! All right. Yesss, all right, okay, this is good, all great." Milia pumped her fist. After clearing her throat, she continued,

"Then would you care to join me while I go out to explore town today?"

"Sure. I wouldn't mind," I agreed.

"Yay! ♪ Then let's meet downstairs in thirty minutes." Milia skipped happily out of the room. "I did it! I did it!"

Her curiously cheery ramblings grew distant as she departed.

I checked how much money I had left.

"..."

I hadn't planned to overstay, so I didn't have much on hand. Would it be enough?

Next, Dey arrived.

"Is something the matter?" I asked her.

"Am I not allowed a visit unless I have some explicit business? I heard from Lord Rileyla that you were still here."

"We're planning to leave tomorrow."

"Then do you have some time this afternoon?"

"I believe I do."

"Oh, marvelous. Would you come to the rocks along the beach sometime in the afternoon? We'll have some fun."

"I can't imagine what you're planning, but all right," I agreed.

"I'm looking forward to it," she said with a wink before leaving.

While I was getting ready to leave, Iris very slowly crept into the room.

"Do you have a moment?"

"Sure. Please come in."

The branch manager glanced to the right and left down the hallway, then quickly slinked inside. "Are you going out?"

"Yes. Miss Milia invited me to look around the town with her."

"Mm-hmm... I—I can't believe her... Making plans with you first thing in the morning...! I can't let her out of my sight...!" Iris muttered to herself with a fraught expression.

"Thank you for everything yesterday at the beach," I said. "It was a good change of pace."

"Was it? I'm glad Rila and Candey enjoyed themselves. You're quite the sly man, surrounding yourself with beautiful women like that. I suppose I shouldn't have expected anything less from our ace employee."

"Ace employee...?" I repeated questioningly.

"That's right. That's how highly everyone thinks of you." Iris laughed for a moment but then turned serious. "Even so, you can't push yourself too hard. Especially since you're still in recovery."

"I know."

Iris apparently had to shadow the local guild branch today, so she bid me good-bye and took her leave. It was just about time for my first appointment, so I went to wait at the inn's entrance. Milia arrived before long, looking very dressed up.

"Th-thank you for waiting. Did I keep you?"

"No. I haven't been here long at all."

"Oh, good... Th-this is almost like a date. It's nice."

Milia led the way, and I followed after as we walked into town. She had said we would be looking around, but I had no idea what that entailed specifically.

"There are rare things from all over sold in the markets here," she explained. "Even window-shopping makes my heart flutter...!"

Milia's eyes glittered as she inspected various arranged curios, evidently enjoying herself. Something caught my eye as well, so I went ahead and bought it.

Bringing a finger to her cheek, Milia wondered aloud, "What shall we eat for lunch? I really wish I could have made something in advance."

I glanced up to check the height of the sun.

Dey said to meet in the afternoon...

Was I already running late?

"Oh, Mr. Roland! There's a seafood place over there!"

When was this going to wrap up? Then again, Milia was really enjoying herself. When I considered that, I felt reluctant to cut this short.

"Let's eat there, then," I decided, adding, "but I need to use the restroom, so please go on ahead first."

"All right, then. I will ♪," she answered.

Having given an excuse, I quickly headed to my next rendezvous.

I was undoubtedly late, but I only needed to convince Dey I wasn't. Once I reached the rocks where I was to meet the undead vampire, I used my Unobtrusive skill.

"I wonder where Master Roland could be...," Dey muttered to herself as she took a seat on a large stone.

"Dey, what are you muttering to yourself about?"

"Oh, Master Roland. You're late, you know."

"I've been here. You just never noticed me."

"Oh my, really? You should have said something."

I'd been trying to figure out what we were going to be doing here when I spotted a rod and some bait at my feet.

I see. So the fun has to involve fishing.

"Well then, let's get started right away," I said.

Nodding, Dey replied, "Yes, let's. Let's reel in a huge haul and have that for dinner tonight."

"All right."

I baited the hook and cast my line. Dey did the same with hers, placed her rod down, and started to kiss me on the cheek.

"We won't have much to do while we wait, will we?" she remarked. "How about...we have a little fun?"

Normally, I wouldn't have minded, but Milia was waiting. This wasn't the time for any tomfoolery. Dey wasn't showing any signs of getting off anytime soon, however.

I reeled in the line and threw it back into the ocean again.

"Hee-hee, Master Roland? No one likes a man who rushes. You need to take your time, see?"

"Everything that lives casts a presence. And it's possible to tell when fish are hungry via that..."

"If catching fish were so easy, no fisherman would come home empty-handed," Dey responded.

I felt a tug on my line.

"I've got one," I stated.

"Seriously?!"

"Please hold the rod. I'll grab the fish so it can't escape."

"You don't need to actually snatch the fish if we're reeling it in—"

"I'll go grab it," I repeated.

After thrusting the fishing pole at Dey, I plunged into the ocean. It wouldn't do for her to pull the thing in right away, so I cast a spell to summon a few shadows. I freed the fish and left my conjured minions to pull on the line.

"Oh dear, oh dear, oh my, oh my. It's a big one. It's pulling back more than before…! It's almost as though something other than a fish is hooked…!"

I activated Unobtrusive again before stealthily setting up a Gate while watching Dey struggle from the corner of my eye. I left the rocks and ran to the shop where Milia was waiting. When I got in, Milia was already seated.

"I'm sorry. I hope I didn't make you wait long."

"Mr. Roland, do you have a stomachache? Are you okay?"

"Yes, well, I suppose I do."

"Oh, um… It's just that you're sopping wet."

"That's from sweat."

"Th-that's a lot of sweat…! Are you sure you're actually feeling better…?"

"It's not a problem. Please don't worry about it."

We both placed our orders, and as we were eating, Milia smacked her lips happily while saying, "This is so yummy."

I heard screeching from outside. When I looked, there was a shadow shaking its head at me and signaling by crossing its arms like an X. Based on its pantomiming, it seemed the tide had washed away several of its kind, and carnivorous fish had eaten others. They wouldn't be able to hold up for much longer.

"Tsk, you're too weak," I muttered.

"Is something wrong?"

"I was just thinking about how frustrated I am by my frail body. I'm sorry. If you could let me leave for a moment..."

"Oh, I see. Would you like me to buy you some medicine?"

"No, please don't worry about me."

I set up a Gate near the restaurant's entrance, and after stopping by a fishery, I made the jump to the rocks.

"This is taking so long...! It's been such a battle! What kind of huge fish must be in there...?! I wonder if Master Roland is all right. He hasn't been coming up to breathe..."

It seemed the remaining shadows were holding their ground.

I headed back into the ocean and hooked the fish onto the line.

"Now!"

Dey tugged on the line, and the store-bought fish went up as Dey jerked it out.

"Oh my, now that's a big fish," she said.

"This seems more than big enough," I observed.

"Master Roland. I suppose things didn't go as well as you'd hoped in the ocean? Hee-hee. Wait... This fish is dead. It's cold, almost as if it had been frozen, and it has dull eyes that look almost exactly like the ones in the market..."

"Dey. This is the result of the struggle to the death you had with it."

"So... It ran out of the strength to live then...? It sure *was* a lengthy fight..." Dey glanced apologetically at the market fish. "Well, then shall we prep it for dinner?"

"Sorry, but I only agreed to fishing. I have something I need to do after this."

"Oh, Master Roland, you're so mean," Dey whined, sticking out her tongue.

"I'll make it up to you," I replied before I made the jump through the Gate back to the restaurant.

After hurrying inside, I found Milia and sat across from her.

"Mr. Roland, how is your stomach feeling? I didn't force you to overextend yourself, did I...?"

"Please don't worry about it," I assured her.

"...? Mr. Roland, that looks a lot like seaweed on your head—"

I quickly flicked it to the ground. It was undoubtedly seaweed, so I concealed it with my foot.

"I suppose it was a bit of trash."

"I—I see...?"

I finished up my cold meal as Milia and I quietly chatted.

We left the restaurant and headed down a different street to look around when we spotted Rila. Next to me, Milia asked with clear resolution, "Mr. Roland, do you have dinner plans?"

"I'm sorry," I answered. "I have something I need to do tonight."

"Y-you do?"

"I was in and out today, though, so I'll treat you to a meal another time," I promised.

Smiling, Milia responded, "Okay. I'm looking forward to that."

No sooner did I part ways with my coworker than Rila approached.

"What are you doing here? Why are you alone?" she inquired.

"You're one to talk, considering you're on your own, too."

"Ha-ha. Incorrect, I am *making* time for myself," Rila boasted for some reason.

I pulled the hair ties I had bought from my pocket and handed them to her. They were decorated with stars and cats and such. "Here. I thought you might be interested in these."

Rila's eyes glittered.

"A-are these for me?! Did you purchase them?"

"I don't really mind if you don't like them," I said.

She quickly snatched hair ties from my hand and shook her head.

"I—I shall make use of them. And I will cherish them..."

It was a relief to know she was pleased with my gift.

"I have discovered an excellent eatery. You surely do not have plans, correct? We shall eat there tonight."

"I thought you might say that," I responded.

Wasting no time, Rila took off. I kept pace beside her.

"I shall treat you as a show of my gratitude. Hee-hee-hee. I suppose I shall not ask why these hair fasteners are wet."

"I'd appreciate if you didn't," I admitted.

Rila immediately bound her locks up with her present. She looked quite pleased with herself and triumphantly hummed. She slipped closer to me and grabbed my hand.

It seemed the restaurant was very far away. We held hands and explored what was nearby as we went. In the end, we headed into a restaurant we had already passed by several times, but I didn't bother questioning why we hadn't gone there immediately.

3
The Scar

Once we finished our activities, Rila let out a breath she'd been holding and started to trace her pointer finger over my skin.

Her finger slipped across my abdomen, skimming along my muscles until it came to an abrupt halt.

She had reached a scar about the size of a pinkie right above my navel.

"Very old…," Rila whispered from on top of the bed. "So even you suffer wounds."

"Of course I do. It wasn't as though I came ready-made from the womb."

Rila gently caressed the ancient injury.

"You have several scars, but this is the only one on the front of your body."

"Yeah," I said.

"…"

It was clear from her expression that Rila wanted to know more about it.

"It isn't an entertaining story," I told her. "I was simply inexperienced. That was it."

"…Oh?"

Though this particular one had long since passed, I still felt some reservations about telling other people about my own errors.

I turned my back to Rila, and she snuggled close from behind, wrapping me with her arms.

"You have them on your shoulders and your back… Stab marks and slashes…"

Rila gently kissed my old wounds. She went over them one by one, breathing out a heavenly breath on each.

I closed my eyes, trying not to remember.

"Sir, could I have a quest?"

On my first day back at work, a girl who had been waiting her turn sat in front of me that busy morning while I was arranging quests for other people.

"Yes, of course. If you could show me your adventurer permit, please," I replied.

I took her permit, which she had laid on the countertop, then started to ask her what kind of job she was looking for.

The girl, Sasha Glideau, was a D-rank adventurer. Eighteen years old. She was your ordinary intermediate-level adventurer. There was nothing special about her.

"…"

It seemed she had grown comfortable with questing and had been taking many D-rank jobs recently.

"It'd be really nice if you could get me something extra-special," she joked, so I gave her a smile.

"I'm not sure we have something that will fit your exact desires... One moment please."

Everyone wanted easy quests that would earn them a lot. Although that was what they all sought, it was rare that an adventurer spoke their mind on the matter.

"What would you think of this?" I asked.

It was guard duty in the mountains.

"Hmm," Sasha hummed.

"The bridge that travelers normally use has been washed away, so they're currently taking detours on an old, narrow road. You'll have to make sure the passage is safe for traveling."

I pulled out a map and gave her a quick explanation. Though we needed many people to help reconstruct the bridge, that task offered little pay and involved difficult work conditions.

"Um, then I just need to protect any who pass by?"

"Yes, if anything happens, we would be counting on you. There are other guilds dispatching adventurers to this region, so I believe everyone will be given different specific roles on-site."

Lord Bardel had also sent his own officials, so I told Sasha to follow their instructions.

"Got it," she answered. "This quest goes on for a while, doesn't it?"

"Until the bridge is repaired."

"I see. Then I'll try it out for a day, and if it works out, I'll come to sign up for it again."

"Very well. Thank you."

Sasha waved and flashed me a cheerful smile before leaving.

Work continued, and my coworkers and I arranged more quests for the adventurers who stopped by and took their reports. It was a fairly busy day.

Suddenly, a young man ran into the guild while shouting, "I-it's a catastrophe!" As he panted and gasped for air, he explained, "A Geht-hawk has appeared on the old road!"

A stir ran through the guild.

Though they normally were not considered high-rank monsters on an individual basis, Geht-hawks were avian ferocities. They were larger than other birds, and when they grew to a certain size, they could occasionally be a challenge for B rankers.

...Or so my employee manual claimed.

"The adventurers on the scene can't handle it. The knights have yet to arrive. Lord Bardel wishes to submit an urgent request!"

Our already hectic day grew even more frantic.

"Make quest stubs."

"What will the reward be?"

"We don't have time to check in with his lordship! What about the rank? It's B rank! B!"

"Do we have anyone around who can immediately take on an emergency quest of that level?!"

As the guild descended into panic, Iris emerged from her office and was quickly apprised of the situation.

Then, when our eyes met, I raised my hand.

"Branch Manager," I called.

"...Yes. Could I ask you to take care of it? The reward and

which adventurers we send out don't matter nearly as much as ensuring the safety of everyone on the scene."

I nodded and headed to the other side of the counter.

Iris clapped her hands together to gather everyone's attention. "All right, please calm down, everyone. Roland is heading out to handle it. Remain calm and return to your regular duties."

When I took a closer look around, I realized that everyone present was at D rank or below. Their fear was understandable.

Some voiced their concern, while others encouraged me.

"Can Roland really manage to fight a large Geht-hawk…?"

"Mr. Roland, give it everything you've got."

"M-Milia's practically got hearts in her eyes…"

"I know the feeling. It's like we're staking all we've got on him. Even my heart skipped a beat…"

I got the particulars from the young man who had rushed in as the adventurers began to stir as well.

"Huh? What? What's going on?"

"Is Mr. Argan going to fight it…?"

"Seriously? Now that's something I've gotta see…"

The horse the young man had come riding on was still hitched in front of the guild. I mounted it as several people stuck their heads out of the windows.

"Huh? Aren't you going to prep in advance?!"

"You're seriously going empty-handed?!?!"

"Don't you need to take something with you?"

I put my hand up to silence the many questions.

"The only thing I need is myself," I told them.

""""H-he's so cool...""""

After nodding slightly, I kicked the horse's sides. I rode through the town, heading straight for the plains.

"You have several wounds, but this is the only one on the front of your body."

Rila's voice echoed in the back of my mind. I tried to silence it by focusing on the task at hand.

A Geht-hawk was a dangerous type of human-eating bird. Depending on its size, it could swallow a person whole. It had appeared along a mountain pass, which wasn't unusual, considering its habitat, but there hadn't been any previous sightings of one there.

My horse galloped along as I guided it on the shortest route I knew. The shrill sound of the Geht-hawk's cry echoed from up ahead. At the same time, I also heard human shrieks. Men who looked like adventurers ran over to me, trying to escape.

"H-help me... What is that bird?"

"This is impossible. We can't handle that thing..."

The two of them fell to their knees, likely from the relief of escaping.

"Hey, do you know what happened to an adventurer named Sasha?" I asked them.

"Hmm? A guild employee...?"

"Sasha... You mean the D-rank girl? She's back there! Way back! She said she'd be able to manage on her own..."

Was she fighting? Perhaps she thought to keep the Geht-hawk at bay until reinforcements arrived.

"Understood."

I urged the horse forward, and it took off running along the mountain pass.

"*Screeeeeeeeeee!*"

When I found the Geht-hawk, it screeched loud enough to be heard throughout the whole region.

Several corpses of adventurers lay on the ground with wounds clearly from a powerful beak. Someone who looked to be a dispatched official was crouching behind the rocks, head in their hands.

"I said get back!" Sasha shouted. The Geht-hawk loudly flapped its wings as she loosed arrows at it. She didn't seem to be much of an archer, however, and her shots failed to find purchase.

"*Screeeeeeeee!*"

"Ahhhhhh!"

As the Geht-hawk swept down on her, Sasha dropped low to evade.

There were cliffs on either side of the road, but they seemed scalable.

"Keep down," I instructed.

"Okay... Wait, aren't you from the guild?!"

I dismounted and picked up one of the swords on the ground, holding it in my mouth. After grabbing a rock, I started to climb up a cliff face.

The Geht-hawk was only going after Sasha. It was frenzied and kept attempting to warn her off.

"I didn't think a Geht-hawk would be too much trouble...but this thing is huge!"

Sasha was practically crying as she threw herself down when the bird swooped at her again. I watched closely, waiting for when the creature tried to gain altitude. When the time was right, I kicked off the wall and held the sword with both hands. With everything I had, I plunged the blade deep into the great bird's body, hoping to bring it down quickly.

"*Kree!*" the Geht-hawk screamed as its blood sprayed, and it tumbled headfirst toward the earth.

"That ended all too quickly," I remarked.

I landed on the ground and stabbed the sword into the dirt.

"Huh? My glasses."

As I'd fallen, they'd come off. They weren't expensive, nor did I actually need them, so I didn't bother trying to find where they'd gotten to.

As I spoke to an official, who was still cowering from a safe place, and explained everything that had happened, Sasha led my horse over by the reins.

"Thank you, sir."

"No need to thank me. It was an emergency."

She stared at me, then grinned.

"With those glasses, I didn't recognize you... But I think this is the second time you've saved me."

"No, I believe this was the first. Maybe you've mistaken me for someone else."

Saying a quick good-bye, I mounted the horse and began the leisurely journey back.

"...So she remembered me."

I arrived back at the guild, my mind occupied with the past.

My coworkers' exclamations created a scene similar to the one when I'd left.

"Huh? Did you really not prep in advance?!"

"Are you sure you went empty-handed?!"

"Did you not need to take anything with you?"

"The only thing I needed was myself."

"That was how it all went down earlier."

Adventurers who hadn't been there when I'd left all applauded.

"""""Mr. Argan is so cool!"""""

◆

It had been my third job as an assassin.

"You better do well, you hear? Keep your head. Adapt to the situation. Got it?"

"..."

All I did was silently nod as Amy ruffled my hair.

I batted her hand away, to which she frowned and said, "Not cute, are ya?"

"If anything doesn't go to plan, you don't panic; you got that? Assume that something will always happen during a job."

As I was prepping my favorite knife, among other things, Amy repeated her warning. I didn't know how many times she'd repeated it to me. I was feeling pretty fed up with it all.

"Understood," I answered. My voice hadn't even broken yet.

Chapter 3   71

It was the same as it'd always been—the same procedures. I'd already memorized the timing, how to sneak in, my escape route. There was no need to worry.

I left the house without a word, running along an animal trail down the mountain. Town was hardly an hour away. I'd have enough time to come back before dawn broke.

Once I got to the capital, I traversed the moat outside the castle and snuck inside through the waterways.

The target's bedroom was easy to reach.

◆

"You're quite popular, Mr. Argan."

Sasha propped her head in her palms on the other side of the counter as she grinned.

It had been several days since the Geht-hawk incident.

Sasha had since settled in this town, coming in every morning to ask me for new quests.

"You truly look completely different without those glasses."

"We do not have a good D-rank quest for you today," I stated. "If you would like an E-rank one, there is a *konsou*-gathering job available. You'll need to gather an herb that is used for healing potions. Personally, I think it's fair work. How does that suit you?"

"All the adventurers say you're an amazing employee and that there's no going wrong taking one of your quests."

"Do they? I feel honored."

"It sure doesn't sound like you do," Sasha quipped with a

laugh. "...So why are you lying?" she pressed. "And why do you bother with the glasses? You don't need them."

"I haven't deceived you about anything. And as for these... I suppose you could say they're part of the look."

They were my disguise, really, but I couldn't tell Sasha that.

"Ah-ha-ha. Your 'look,' huh? Then I'll take that *konsou*-gathering quest."

"As you wish."

I handled the usual clerical work and explained the area where Sasha would have to go, any monsters she might need to face, and the ways to manage them.

"If you come against an unexpected threat like the other day, please run away."

"I know, I know," she replied. "Despite the way I look, I'm still a D ranker. Are you a worrywart, Mr. Argan?"

"No. I only say this to people who are likely to be reckless or make a mistake."

"Oh! That's so mean of you! Are you assuming I'll make a mistake, Mr. Argan?"

"You're holding up the next person in line, so please take care as you leave."

"Ugh! Okay, I get it."

Sasha pouted visibly, but she left the guild with a wave and a smile.

"I'll finish up this quest real quick and be back before you know it," she declared prior to exiting.

While I was taking care of a female adventurer waiting her

turn, Milia asked me a question from the next counter over, where she was working.

"You seem to really get along with Sasha. I thought she just moved here."

"Yes, it seems she's taken a liking to me, although I'm not entirely sure why."

"Sh-she's not a stalker, is she? Mr. Roland, please tell me if you ever find yourself in trouble."

"It's nothing quite that serious. I'll be fine."

Milia tilted her head to the side. "You think so? Hmm... Then again, I guess anyone would take a liking to you if you bravely dashed in to save them."

"You're overthinking it," I responded, then returned my attention to the papers on my desk.

I honestly wished Sasha would move along to another town. I'd thought she was dead—or a slave, at the very least. Now that I saw her every day, I couldn't help but wonder what had happened, even though I didn't want to know. There was no helping my curiosity.

Milia was supposed to come over tonight to teach Rila how to cook.

The workday neared conclusion without anything out of the ordinary happening.

"It's the best when things are normal... I always make mistakes and get worked up when it gets hectic...," Milia muttered, and I wholeheartedly agreed.

Normal was the best.

Wise words, indeed.

Yet as closing time neared, Sasha hadn't shown up.

"Miss Sasha said she would be back immediately after finishing the quest," I said.

"Hmm... Maybe she finished the quest, but she's waiting to report on it until tomorrow?" posited Milia.

That seemed plausible.

There were many adventurers like that. However, they typically reported back on the same day for gathering and slaying quests. Any time they spent sleeping, in their lodgings or in taverns, was just more time their deliverables could be stolen.

Theft was apparently common in the cheap taverns that adventurers tended to frequent. Thus, guilds in larger settlements remained open twenty-four hours. Ever since I'd made the switch into this occupation, I'd become warier of others endangering themselves. That was why I'd been more careful advising adventurers who seemed foolhardy, even when all I had to go off was a hunch.

Closing time arrived, and we locked up from inside. After Iris thanked us all for our efforts, we departed for our homes.

"Are you worried about Sasha?" Milia asked.

"She went *konsou* gathering... The woods are close by, so I'm going to check on her," I answered.

"What? Are you sure she hasn't come back to town?"

"I don't mind making sure."

Some people are simply born unlucky. Sasha was probably one such example. Misfortune had befallen her back in the day, too.

"Oh, but Mr. Roland!" Milia yelled as I ran, but I didn't pay her any heed.

I borrowed one of the guild horses at the stables and rode off.

While the forest wasn't deep, being so unremarkable as to have no name, I could tell there was something wrong. There were people deeper in.

"..."

I hitched my horse at the edge of the woods and entered.

They made no effort to conceal themselves, so I knew my opponents were not going to be anything challenging. I kept my footsteps light as I pursued them.

"So what're we doin' with the girlie?"

"Her face don't look half bad."

Voices were debating something as orange firelight bled from between the trees.

"A D-rank adventurer... It only took a blow to the back of the head to knock her out."

"D rankers are wannabes. After we have our fun with her, we can sell her to the slave merchants."

From the shadows, I scanned the area and spied two men who looked like bandits. Sasha was with them, splayed out in front of the fire. She looked unconscious.

"Well, she's an adventurer. I betchu all kinds of men have bedded her."

"What's another two? She can't complain about that."

Lewd smiles flitted across the men's faces as they pulled off their pants and underwear.

"She might wake up."

"Struggling's appealing in its own way."

I held pieces of the blazing kindling in either hand and thrust them into their exposed asses.

Sizzle.

""Gaaaaaaaaah?!""

"I'm responsible for that adventurer," I told them. "I can't have you hurting her."

"Wh-who the hell are you?!"

"Does it matter? Beat it."

I crouched down and checked Sasha's eyes.

"Or would you like me to chop those off for you and feed them to the fire?"

"Yeek!"

The bandit pair shook their heads with tears in their eyes. The blood rushed out of more than just their heads.

They were trivial—it wasn't even worth killing the ruffians.

I burned them again, and they took off shrieking, still undressed. They'd likely end up arrested by the knights, but that was a separate matter.

I picked up Sasha and headed to the edge of the woods. She was still out cold. The only injury I could see was the bump on the back of her head.

I got onto the horse with Sasha seated in front of me, and we set off for town.

"Hmm... Huh...? I'm not in the woods...?"

"Are you awake? You hit your head and lost consciousness," I explained.

"Mr. Argan…? Why…? I was in the middle of a quest…"

"I had a feeling something bad might have happened to you."

"You've saved me again. This is the third time."

"No, it's the second."

Upon reaching town, I returned the horse, then took Sasha back to her lodgings. There was a look in her eyes that invited me to stay, but I pretended to be ignorant of it. Sasha grabbed my sleeve, as though she'd made up her mind about something. When I brushed her off, she seemed shocked.

"Can't you…stay with me? E-even just for one night. I want to thank you…"

"I'm fine. I didn't save you for that."

If I struck up any relations with her, she was sure to stay in Lahti. Then she would come to me every morning and force me to remember the past, whether she realized it or not.

I bowed slightly and left.

◆

My third mark had been a merchant.

When he came back to his mansion in the capital, I snuck into his house without a sound.

"Supposedly, he doesn't deal in very respectable goods. Although that's to be expected if someone wants him dead," Amy had told me.

Who my target was didn't matter to me. It was just another job to carry out.

It was only when I reached the target's bedroom that I realized how true Amy's reminder to assume something would go wrong during an assassination was.

The man I had been tasked with killing was already dead.

◆

After I'd rescued Sasha, I returned home and was greeted by a table lined with dishes Milia and Rila had prepared together. Rila's face lit up upon seeing me.

"You are late," she said. "Milia informed me you might be, though you were quicker about it than I expected."

"Yes. I had a personal matter to attend to."

Rila tilted her head, seeming doubtful. Milia had already gone home, so Rila regaled me with their cooking escapades while I ate. Hearing and seeing her felt like a relief. The house, the way the furniture was set up—it all reminded me I was living here.

Perhaps my thoughts showed on my face because Rila remarked, "You seem to have had something on your mind recently. You may tell me about it, if you desire. Was it Iris? Was she belligerent with you?" Rila laughed at her own joke. "Regardless, if you would like to speak about it, I am willing to lend you an ear."

Despite her way of putting it, I knew that Rila was curious about what troubled me. It wasn't the sort of thing to share over a meal, however, so I quickly finished up, and we headed to the living room.

We opened a bottle of wine and picked at the leftovers from dinner as we sipped from our glasses.

"Does it concern something personal?" questioned Rila.

"More or less," I answered.

She wasn't teasing me anymore. The former demon lord picked at some boiled chicken and audibly chugged her drink.

"You may consult me about it," she declared. Although she was acting high and mighty, the woman simply wanted to know.

"The scar on my abdomen... I got that on a mission. It was during my third job."

Rila rubbed my stomach from her spot next to me.

"So you made an error, then? I am sure it must have smarted," she commented, almost treating me as though I were a child.

Well, at the time, I was.

Back then, I'd been far too overconfident.

"I don't know exactly how old I was, but my teacher decided the day I was taken in would be my fifth birthday. It was six years after that, so I was about eleven."

"Hmm?"

Rila seemed surprised, but I continued anyway.

"My target was a merchant—one wealthy enough to afford a mansion in the capital."

Based on what I had heard after the fact, he amassed his wealth via coercive means and had several grudges with others to show for it.

"He was distributing weapons to insurgents in secret at the time," I explained.

Rila frowned. "What a dangerous man. At times, a person with riches can be more frightening than one with soldiers."

That was likely why someone wanted him dead.

"Yes, I see," Rila continued. "So you attempted to kill that merchant, but he fought back and hurt you?"

"Not even close. Listen until the end."

"Ngh."

"When I tried to kill him, he was already dead."

"Oh?"

"The timing for everything had been wrong."

Truthfully, the failure could have been chalked up to my lack of experience at the time. Another assassin had snuck into the room as I had and slew the merchant first.

"Both of us were startled, but he regained his composure before I could. He realized what I was there for and knew he had to keep me quiet. I hadn't lifted a finger, but my work was already done. Honestly, I should have simply left."

Looking back on it, I realized that logically that was all I'd needed to do, but I hadn't been able to process what had happened at the time.

It was only my third assassination job. Amy's cautioning had all been for nothing. I hadn't been able to adapt.

Rila sipped at her glass as she quietly listened.

"The whole thing was truly a mess. Before either of us made a move, the door opened slowly. There was a girl even younger than I standing there, hoping to sleep with her father.

That had shaken me up considerably. However, I came to my senses when I detected the other assassin's hostility.

"He thought she was an inconvenience and tried to kill her. I moved to meet him without thinking. As I recall, our strength was about equal, although honestly, I can't be sure anymore... My knife was sticking out of his chest, and his was buried in my stomach."

I was lucky my opponent hadn't struck higher. It was also fortunate that the other assassin was smaller than I'd first believed. Or perhaps it was merely that his hand had slipped in the surprise.

The agony had been so intense I thought my mind was going to split in two.

"In the end, I killed the person who offed my target instead of the person I was supposed to take out."

"And that is what resulted in this wound?" Rila caressed the scar from over my clothes.

"I returned home injured, and my teacher scolded me while patching me up. I can't recall what she said, but I know she was furious."

"But she still saved you."

Of course, I'd known about the family, but understanding information held an entirely different weight than seeing them in person.

"If I'd been two minutes—no, even just a minute sooner, I would have been the one to kill her father."

"You were not, however."

"Yes. But there was only a slight difference."

"And thanks to it, a little girl survived," Rila said, but I shook my head.

I hadn't felt like a savior at the time.

"...I was overtaken by the guilt."

I was a child not yet familiar with his own line of work. My teacher explained to me what happened to the merchant's family later on. Once it came to light that he had been peddling weapons to rebels, his family was cast into poverty.

"So then that girl who has been so infatuated with you is the child you aided years ago..."

"Yes. I'm surprised you know about that."

"Milia informed me."

"Had I remained an assassin, I likely would have forgotten all about it."

"Hmm. I see... So you are atoning for your crime, then?"

"I suppose you could call it that. Maybe it's because I've recently come to learn what warmth, loneliness, and love feel like."

Rila exhaled heavily. Her breath reeked of alcohol. "Why is it that you feel guilty for another person's misdeeds? Why must you be the one to make amends for them, knave? I believe it was a good thing you rescued her..."

"When I see someone right in front of me... When I can see that they're in danger, I can't help but want to save them... I'm not an assassin anymore."

"If that makes you feel better, then I do not see an issue." Rila flipped my clothes up and started to caress my scar directly. "So even you have been stabbed."

"Just in the past. I've never taken a hit on the chest since."

Rila patted my head. "It is good of you to put serious consideration into this… But overthinking will accomplish nothing."

"…"

I looked at the wine bottle. At some point, it had been emptied. Rila had evidently only kept quiet while I was talking because of the drink.

"…I am glad to learn more about you and know that I can be closer to you…," she admitted as she inched nearer and embraced me. "Please tell me more about yourself, more things no one else knows… No matter what you have done, I am always on your side."

I stroked Rila's crimson hair.

She had latched on to me tight and was showing no sign of relinquishing, so I picked her up in my arms and brought her to bed.

"It seems very odd to carry the demon lord like a princess," I commented.

"What are you going on about? I was originally the princess of my kin. You would do well to treat me so. P-please be gentle tonight…"

Her words sank to such a strange whisper that I laughed slightly.

"Mr. Argan, please."

"What can we do for you today?"

Hearing someone mention my name, I glanced over to find Sasha and Milia sitting on opposite sides of the counter.

"I'd like a quest. So I'd like Mr. Argan, please," Sasha repeated.

"I can also arrange jobs for you," replied Milia. Her classic work smile felt a bit more intense than usual today.

Typically, she showed no qualms about calling me over, yet she refused to leave her seat this time. She wasn't matching the adventurer with a quest so much as having it out with the other young woman.

It appeared I wasn't the only one to pick up on her change of tone. My coworkers all had as well and were watching things play out.

"But Mr. Argan is right there."

"He is, but I'm afraid he's busy with many other matters."

Was I actually that unavailable? I was just organizing adventurer applications and checking how many unfulfilled quests we had. It was all standard documentation work. Truthfully, I was already half done. Some counter duty wouldn't have been an issue at all.

However, Milia had more experience than I did. If she declared I was too busy, then it must have been so.

"Oh? Isn't that the baby who's been coming in a lot lately?" Maurey blurted out.

Baby?

""""*Baby?*"""""

I wasn't the only one bothered by that word. All the other staffers who had heard Maurey's statement appeared just as ruffled.

Two female guild workers were whispering to each other about the situation.

"Looks like Milia has finally lost her patience."

"She's been so bothered by that adventurer's frequent meetings with Roland."

Approaching the pair because they seemed to know what was going on, I inquired, "Um. Why is Miss Milia not turning her over to me today?"

The women exchanged a look.

"Well..."

"About that..."

"An adventurer can get hurt or killed during quests. I think it's only natural they would want jobs from people they trust and rely on," I stated matter-of-factly.

""Oh, Argan...""

The two of them gave me somewhat exasperated looks.

"That's not what the girl's thinking about at all."

"I'm not keen on mixing personal stuff with work, but I do understand how she feels."

...I couldn't comprehend what they meant in the slightest. It seemed like the most efficient way to get the work done was for Milia to turn Sasha's case over to me.

"I'd like Mr. Argan to arrange my quest, though," Sasha insisted.

"All you've been talking about is Mr. Argan. I thought you came here for work," Milia shot back.

Sasha scowled, clicking her tongue in irritation. "That's right. And I've been saying I'd like Mr. Argan to arrange that job this whole time."

"Please show me your adventurer permit, and I'll assign one for you."

"Don't you get it?! I'm only going to show it to Mr. Argan!"

"Can you just admit you're solely here to see Mr. Roland?"

Sasha and Milia's back-and-forth was starting to become heated.

We had few clients today and many staff members without much to do, but instead of stopping Milia, they were content to watch the show.

"What is with you? Ugh, fine. I did come to see him!" Sasha admitted at last.

"Then you're mixing work with your private life! That's inadvisable!" chided Milia.

Huh? Looking around, I saw that my coworkers were giving Milia dubious looks. Their expressions all but said, *You're one to talk.*

"Milia's always following him around like a puppy, and now she's standing her ground against a rival love interest."

"She sure has grown up, although she's become quite the hypocrite in the process."

The female employees were smiling as they observed Milia's crusade. Since Milia was the youngest guild staffer, all our colleagues had taken a liking to her.

Maurey breathed out a long sigh.

"Hey there, baby. None of this is a good idea, you know. Your crush on that rookie doesn't bother me, but this is a branch of the Adventurers Guild. You come here to get quests and to report back on them. It's no place to request specific guild employees to cater to you. You got that?"

Maurey had come to Milia's aid by doing what he did best—arguing.

Yet neither of the women embroiled in battle spared Maurey so much as a glance, content to keep bickering.

"Huh... Are you ignoring me?"

The two of them kept at it, shunning Maurey as he stood there dumbfounded.

"The other staff members have been calling you Mr. Roland's stalker!" declared Milia.

"B-but that's not my intention," Sasha quickly denied.

"Whether you mean to or not, it's hard to see your actions as anything else."

The female guild employees standing behind Milia shook their heads with reproachful looks.

"No one's been calling her a stalker, Milia..."

"You're the only one who's been worrying and making a fuss..."

They were right. From behind me, a pair of male coworkers offered their own thoughts on the situation in hushed voices.

"Looks like Maurey's trying to pounce on another opportunity."

"What do you mean?"

"All the adventurer gals who've got their eyes on Roland are pretty."

"Yeah, well, I suppose. Some of them are kind of Goody Two-shoes, but he's even got really showy fans, too."

"Right, and Maurey's after them. He's out to get the cute

ones in their late teens and early twenties. When Roland's not on counter duty, he's always over there trying to chat them up."

"Whoa, now that's sleazy..."

"Right? He's already asked five or six women out to dinner, and he's been turned down every time. He refused to stop, though, so they've had to find work with other guild branches."

"I thought I'd been seeing less of some people lately, but I had no clue that was why... That Sasha's pretty cute, too."

"You hadn't heard? I thought everyone knew."

This was the first I'd heard of it as well.

I didn't care whether Maurey was hitting on people, but doing so to the point that adventurers felt uncomfortable was not something I could condone.

"Heeeey! Stop ignoring me!" Maurey cried, which finally got Milia and Sasha to look at him.

"Mr. Maurey, can you please keep it down?"

"Stay out of this, old man."

"O-old?" Maurey pursed his lips as he made a displeased sound. "I'm not old! A-and quit being so clingy!"

The outburst earned a few questioning looks from other staffers. *You're one to talk*, their eyes said. Evidently, everyone was thinking the same thing...again.

"Go after someone too much, and they might send their scary lover after you...," Maurey stated.

""""He's gotta be talking from experience.""""

Even after such an embarrassing event, he probably didn't intend to mend his ways.

"And sometimes people'll start talking behind your back."

"""""...So he knows."""""

I had to wonder why Maurey kept hitting on female adventurers when he knew that doing so was so risky.

"By the way...I'm speaking from direct experience."

"""""Obviously."""""

Maurey appeared as though he'd managed to hurt his own feelings with his words. He turned around, looking depressed as can be. I watched him beat a weary retreat to his desk in the back.

Despite Maurey's interruption, Milia and Sasha's argument showed no signs of letting up. Even adventurers who had wandered in midway were watching.

During the course of it all, I'd even finished the work that had rendered me "too busy."

"Miss Milia, I'm free now, so I can handle Sasha's request," I said.

"Mr. Roland... But she—"

Milia hardly seemed keen on my offer. Sasha pointed a finger at her and snorted triumphantly. "Well, miss, Mr. Argan is here, so your presence is no longer required."

"Grrr......"

Milia eyed Sasha uneasily and wore an expression that suggested she wished to say more, but she voiced no further resistance. I motioned Sasha over and had her take a seat before sitting down myself.

"So it seems you're not here for a quest," I remarked.

Suddenly appearing uncomfortable, Sasha averted her gaze as she asked, "…You heard that?"

"Yes. With how vehemently you were arguing, everyone did."

"I'm sorry. If I was getting in the way of work, I'll apologize. I just needed to speak with you." Sasha didn't even bother to take out her adventurer permit. She just cast her eyes downward and stared. "I recognize that I might have been a little too persistent, just like that other employee said. But don't worry. I won't involve myself with you anymore, Mr. Argan."

"…What do you mean?"

"I'm going to be moving on to another town."

"I see," I answered indifferently, which brought a strained smile to Sasha's face.

"You really don't care at all."

"The adventurers we serve are free to do as they wish."

"I think I understand why the others are so desperate to get your attention. When someone tries to pull you in, you want to push them away, and when they're trying to get away, you want to follow after them. Still, you're so kind."

The office had grown strangely quiet. All present were undoubtedly eavesdropping.

"Let's go somewhere else," I told Sasha before standing.

I didn't want her offering any careless remarks that might invite the curiosity of my coworkers, considering she knew about my past. I led Sasha out behind the Adventurers Guild, where there were fewer people around.

"So you came today to report that you'll be moving to another branch?" I asked.

"That's right. I won't be stopping in to see you anymore, and I wanted you to know," she replied. It had felt like she had moved past me since I'd turned down her offer to spend the night with her. "You saved me in the past, so—"

"No, that wasn't me...," I said.

"I know why you were there that night, Mr. Argan. But it's all right. You saved me regardless. That's the truth. And you've come to my rescue two more times since. I started to think it might be fate, so I tactlessly propositioned you..."

It had been a rather forward invitation. Judging by Sasha's hesitation and how inexperienced she seemed, it had likely taken all the courage she could muster.

"I hope you'll disregard that as the rash words of a girl stuck in daydreams and fairy tales." Sasha let an easy laugh tumble out of her mouth before continuing, "I thought about things a lot that night you left me alone. I'm an adventurer, and you're a guild worker—nothing more. I'm not the daughter of some great merchant anymore, and you're not the savior who arrived in the dark. I've been trying to dredge up a past that we've already abandoned."

After her father's misdeeds had come to light, Sasha's family had been cast from the higher echelons of society, and she'd been orphaned.

"I don't need that history, not as an adventurer. I've decided, somewhat selfishly, to say good-bye, and I came here to tell you as much."

Just as Sasha was a reminder of life from when I was a kid, I was a symbol of her younger days, too.

"Do you have any plans from here on out?" I inquired.

With a mischievous smile, Sasha replied, "Are you interested in knowing? Sorry, I don't have any set route. None at all. I might be done in by monsters tomorrow, or fate might intervene, and I could find someone and wind up a mother. Anything is possible."

She was open to any eventuality.

"I'm an adventurer, after all!"

I nodded, then Sasha, blushing, offered me her hand.

"Thank you, my hero, and...good-bye."

"Good luck to you."

I took Sasha's hand for a moment, then she turned away and started to run. I watched as she disappeared, growing smaller in the distance, then I heard the sound of someone exhaling a long-held breath.

When I turned around, I spotted Iris watching me from the back entrance.

"Were you eavesdropping?" I questioned.

"I was. Sorry. Milia was insistent. '*Branch Manager, Mr. Roland is toooo popular!*' she said."

Iris's impression of Milia was pretty spot-on.

"She's distracted and having trouble with her work, so I thought it would be a good idea to apprise her on everything that happened," Iris explained.

"I can set her straight on the details," I offered.

Impersonating Milia again, Iris replied, "*'She has to be his ex, Branch Managerrr!'* She was about to cry. Please see to it quickly."

She mimicked Milia so accurately that I could practically see the scene unfolding before my eyes.

"I will," I answered.

"Also, please don't mix your private life with work."

"There's someone who needs to hear that more than me, Branch Manager."

With a look of surprise, Iris questioned, "Oh? Who?"

4
Consultation

"Uh, excuse me!"

For once, I was helping a male adventurer. Immediately, I noticed he was acting unusually.

"Yes? Are you looking for a quest today?" I asked.

"N-no. I-I'm not here for that…"

The young man didn't even look twenty. He could have easily been described as a boy. Gazing at him, I asked what was going on.

"…Um… So, Melissa…"

I didn't recall the woman's face very well, but I did remember arranging a quest for an adventurer by that name recently.

"Please stop looking at her funny! J-just because the girls like you doesn't mean you can ogle her! M-Melissa's got me!"

While I pondered how best to reply, an intermediate adventurer I recognized inserted himself into the conversation.

"'Scuse me, kid. What're you talking to the boss for? You got business with him?" Neal placed a firm hand on the younger man's shoulder, a shallow smile on his face.

Neal's friend, Roger, sidled up and took the other shoulder.

"Hey there, kid... If you have something to say to the boss, you gotta go through us first. Understand?"

"Yeek! I'm not looking for trouble... I-it's more that I'm asking him something..."

The young adventurer was so intimidated by the pair that he was practically shrinking before our eyes.

"Boss, we're gonna teach this ignorant kid a little lesson." Neal dragged the young man away by the collar.

"Please let him go. I'd like to hear what he has to say, at least," I stated.

Admittedly, I didn't recall doing anything to this Melissa, so the accusation seemed like a false one to me.

Neal released the young man, who collapsed into his seat.

"You better not say anything scummy about the boss."

"Please don't threaten him," I requested.

"Yessir, sorry!"

"I'm not the one you should apologize to," I added.

Neal and Roger scratched their heads awkwardly, then expressed their remorse. Then they headed over to an open counter in order to accept a quest.

They'd been acting no different than bullies.

Looking to the young man, I said, "My apologies for their actions."

"I-it's okay..."

Despite his reply, the boy was still clearly on edge.

"Has something happened to Miss Melissa? You said I was looking at her oddly."

"I'm sorry… I got carried away…"

"It's all right. You haven't offended me."

The young man finally introduced himself as Gil, a new E-rank adventurer.

I see. So this is Gil.

"Melissa is from my village, too, and we struck out as adventurers together."

"She's an E ranker, too, correct?" I asked.

"…Yes. At first, she just wanted an excuse to leave home, but she didn't have money. Taking quests was supposed to be a way to earn spending money… Recently, however, she's gotten really into the job."

"Isn't that a good thing?"

Admittedly, I was having trouble seeing the issue.

"It is, but… Apparently her passion springs from interest in a really cool guy working the front desk here. She wants to do well because he praises her, and when she has difficulty, he helps figure out why and devises strategies with her…"

"What a considerate worker," I remarked, impressed. That was exactly how I envisioned the ideal guild employee. In my line of work, one needed to motivate adventurers and aid them when they had trouble.

"I'm talking about you!"

Smacking my knee, I exclaimed, "Oh, I see!"

"So um… I'd like to ask you not to see her, even if she asks for you…"

That was a difficult request. Helping people like Melissa was my job, and part of that was providing motivation to complete quests. Gil was being rather selfish, and I had no obligation to obey. Suddenly, I realized why he might be doing this.

"Mr. Gil, are you jealous of me?"

"..."

The young man went stone-faced.

I'd clearly hit the mark.

A boy and girl at a delicate age had left home together and were living as adventurers. Of course he was interested in her.

"So you've known each other from childhood, I take it?" I asked.

"Huh? Oh yes. That's right."

"Have you told Melissa about this?"

"No... I haven't mentioned it. And it wouldn't seem cool for her to know I'm jealous..."

Perhaps it was unexpected, but women were often pleased to know that a guy was envious.

"I think you should tell her how you feel."

"Wha...? But that's basically the same as confessing that I like her..."

"Don't you, though?"

"Uh... Well, that's true, but..."

Gil was becoming embarrassed.

How very innocent. They both were.

"If you can tell her, then I'll do as you ask and won't work with Miss Melissa even when she comes by. Does that work for you?"

"Y-yes..."

Milia giggled from behind me. I turned around and placed a

finger against my lips. After offering Gil a bit of encouragement, I sent him on his way.

"I'm so looking forward to that. My heart is fluttering just wondering what'll happen between the two of them...!" Milia was very excited.

From what I understood, Gil and Melissa were very alike, so I was sure it would be fine.

Several days passed, and Gil stopped by to thank me.

"Thank you so much, sir. When I came clean to her about my feelings, Melissa admitted she felt the same way..."

Melissa, who stood beside Gil, bowed rather bashfully to me.

"Excuse me, sir, could I talk to you about something? It's about the boy I left the village with..."

Melissa had come to the Adventurers Guild to speak with me in the past, but it had been about Gil.

The two were holding hands and looked to be on cloud nine.

"Are you dating? Congratulations!" Milia exclaimed, pushing me to the side.

"Um, yes... We came by to thank Mr. Argan for helping us get together."

The two had known each other their entire lives and had left home together. Gil hadn't been the only one interested in the other.

"I just...feel like he thinks of me as a younger sister..."

Melissa had evidently misunderstood. So I'd told her to try acting like she was interested in another man to see how Gil would react.

…Admittedly, I hadn't expected her to pick me.

Still, it had worked instantly. Melissa had never been keen on living as an adventurer. That was Gil's dream. She'd known that her feelings would remain unrequited if she stayed in their village, so she'd followed after Gil.

Head still lowered, Melissa said, "We're so indebted to you."

"Please don't worry about it. I'm just happy it worked out. I guess this means you're not merely childhood friends anymore."

""Yes.""

The pair were so embarrassingly soppy.

Neal and Roger watched with eyes like dead fish.

"Chile-hood free-ends? What's that?" Neal questioned.

"I dunno… Sounds like a new type of monster…," Roger replied.

"Luh-vers…gee-url-free-end… What are those again…?"

"I dunno… Sounds like a new type of monster…," Roger repeated.

Gil and Melissa laughed bashfully and left.

"I'm sure those two will give all their future quests their best effort," I remarked.

Milia exuberantly watched the happy couple depart.

"It's wonderful… They're both working to make the other happy. How absolutely splendid."

I truly wished the best for them.

"Boss… How do I get popular with the ladies?"

"You have no sense of hygiene, Mr. Neal, so I recommend cleaning yourself up. Please start by shaving off that stubble."

"Y-yessir…!"

"But, Neal, you said that stubble's a manly affectation!"

"Sh-shut up! You better not stop me!"

After witnessing the unusual occurrence, the other adventurers present all lined up at my counter.

Most of the adventurers I worked with were women, but from that day forward, I gained a bunch of male clients.

"H-how can I get girls to like me, sir?"

For a while, my work felt more like giving love advice than arranging quests.

5
Ride the Tide

After our office was destroyed by the explosion, it was repaired, and some features, like the entrance and reception counter, were renovated. Maybe that was why we had so many adventurers crowding the place in the days following our reopening.

On one particular day, the area chief came for an inspection, and an unease hung about the office all the while.

The area chief was a woman in her late thirties who wore rimless glasses.

She oversaw all the guilds in the region. There were four regions in total, one for each cardinal direction, with the capital at the center where they met. Basically, she outranked even Iris.

The area chief had been looking over documents in an office and watching us work. Her mannerisms were rather refined, which led me to believe she came from the aristocracy. The Adventurers Guild system had originally been created by nobles, in fact. Higher positions were more frequently held by the wealthy.

"Ms. Iris?"

"Y-yes?"

When the area chief called her, Iris hastened to the woman's side, trying to deduce what the issue might be.

"Is it always this busy in here?"

"No, we've only recently reopened since reconstructing after the accident."

"Are you sure it's not merely due to your incompetence?"

"S-sorry?"

"Are you certain that your suboptimal teaching skills haven't resulted in your employees all being worse at their jobs?"

The area chief was loudly laying on the accusations as she scolded Iris. It was as though she wanted the employees to hear.

"And to think you just received a commendation from the headquarters."

When I tried to ask something, Milia whispered to me, "Apparently the lady with the glasses is from a guild that was regularly praised by the guild master."

"I see. So this is because we got the prize this time."

"Uh-huh, that's right. I don't think she was too pleased about that."

The bespectacled area chief turned and leveled her gaze squarely at us.

"You're busy, and yet you have enough time for idle chitchat."

"S-sorry..."

Iris hurriedly bowed her head several times.

"You're completely right, Area Chief! I've often thought the same thing about our performance. We're not doing too hot, I'd say. It's not surprising you picked up on that!" Deciding to suck up,

Maurey agreed with everything the area chief said. Some things never changed.

"Tsk." One of my coworkers clucked their tongue.

"Tsk."

"Tsk."

"Tsk."

"Tsk, tsk."

"Don't get so carried away."

A chorus of dramatic disapproval sounded in reply to Maurey.

"Area Chief, why don't we move along to a quieter place, like the reception room? I'll prepare you some tea."

Maurey wore the smuggest look on his face he'd had in the last three months as he motioned with his thumb for her to follow him to the reception room.

"And what are you doing, then?"

"Huh? I'm...being hospitable to an important guest..."

"I have no need for tea. Can't you see how busy your coworkers are? Well, I'm sure they're all busy because they're reaping what they've sown. Have you no urge to assist?"

"Oh, uh, um..."

When Iris saw Maurey floundering, she placed a hand to her forehead.

"Maurey, please help at the reception counter and with the appraisal."

"Y-yes, ma'am..." He did an about-face and headed to his task. "The hero makes a fashionably late entrance... Am I right?"

No one really understood what he was getting at.

"Everything will be fine if you leave it to me. What should I do? Tell me whatever you need," Maurey added.

With how busy we were, the area chief's indirect prodding, and Maurey's antics, everyone was ready to burst from irritation. While attending to their work, my colleagues piled on the requests for Maurey.

"Why don't you make some tea?"

"Why don't you pay a courtesy call to that woman in the glasses, huh?"

"We don't need a hero when we've got Roland."

"You're the embarrassment of this branch office, Mr. Maurey."

I thought Milia had the most scathing remark, personally.

"...Give today your best effort, everyone," Maurey said, flashing a smile and heading off to the bathrooms. Little tears were forming in his eyes. What had happened to the hero?

"Ms. Iris, this is why you must run a tight ship."

"Y-yes, ma'am. You're completely right..."

After that, Iris had to listen to the area chief pick her apart at length.

"Nine o'clock? For your opening hour? Rather lax, don't you think? Since you're so inefficient, you should open up much earlier."

"But the adventurers in this town aren't awake at eight..."

"My guild in Elise, which is under my direct supervision, starts work at eight. And we only close after midnight."

Elise was the largest city to the west of the capital. It and Lahti were in the same region.

"Well… That's because the towns are different sizes… And the branches also have a different number of employees."

"You certainly have no shortage of excuses," the bespectacled area chief replied as she pushed up her glasses. "A commendation from the guild master is no excuse to rest on your laurels."

"We aren't…"

I mostly comprehended what the lady with the glasses was thinking. She definitely hadn't been pleased when our branch had received a public acknowledgment. However, she was likely more concerned that Iris was a potential threat to her positon. Any achievement our branch made while under her stewardship would bolster her professional standing.

"If that's how you feel, then I have a few more things to correct you on," the area chief spat.

"I didn't intend to imply you were wrong—"

"Please stop talking. There are plenty of people ready to take your place!" yelled the area chief, now almost in hysterics.

That was more than an idle threat. There were only a few area chiefs in the entire Adventurers Guild; she undoubtedly had the power to get a branch manager in a little town fired.

The room went quiet, and both the staffers and adventurers looked up from what they were doing.

"I came here for an inspection because I heard this guild did good work, and what do I find? Mediocre performance and a branch manager who only knows how to complain."

"…W-we're not mediocre! P-please stop putting down my employees!" Iris gathered up her courage. Her fists were trembling.

"Plant your head to the ground right now, right here and take back what you said. Do that, and I may forgive you." Raising a finger, the area chief jabbed it threateningly at the ground.

Iris shook her head, however.

"I—I have never in my entire tenure thought that any of my employees did subpar work! So I won't go back on what I said, and I won't be bowing, either."

"Ohhh, is that right? Looks like you'll be going back to working the floor then."

I sighed.

Milia tugged at my uniform as she observed the scene.

"Mr. Roland, that look on your face is scaring me. Y-you can't, okay? I know you're planning on saying something. She'll kick you out!"

However, I brushed off Milia's comment and headed toward Iris and the bespectacled woman.

"Area Chief, the reason Iris objected to the way you do things is because each town has its own needs. We operate differently to cater to the needs of Lahti."

"What are you getting at?"

"I mean to say that what you've proposed isn't sensible."

"Evidently, you don't want to keep your job."

"Roland," Iris objected.

"Just keep quiet."

"Oh, okay..."

"Area Chief, there are plenty of people who can replace *you* as well."

"Of all the things a lowly staffer could say. You're fired! Fired, you hear me?!"

A stir ran through the guild.

"If you say so... By the way, have you heard about the new tactical adviser positions?"

"Of course. The guild master told me that he has someone he trusts in this region who—"

I showed the area chief my bonus as well as the official appointment letter I'd received along with it.

"That would be me," I stated.

"What? Is that...real?"

As she read over the appointment letter, the woman's face turned pale.

"I tried to turn him down several times, but the guild master begged me, and I took the job because I wasn't given any other choice. Regretfully, the guild master may have no recourse but to terminate you for insulting me."

"Um, excuse me, wait just one moment! I take it back! I take what I said earlier back!"

"Thank you. I'm happy we could come to an understanding. In that case..." I pointed at the ground. "Please plant your head to the floor, right here. Do that, and I'll forgive you."

The area chief furiously chewed her lower lip. "Grrr..."

"I've known the guild master for a long time... You could say we're as thick as thieves..."

Truthfully, we hadn't spent that much time together, but that hardly mattered.

"What do you think will happen when the guild master hears about all your false accusations? How do you like the idea of working your way up from the bottom all over again?" I needled.

The lady with glasses gave a strange strangled sound. After a moment, she begrudgingly stated, "I-it seems there's nothing wrong with this guild branch." With that, she made a quick exit.

Everyone present except for me let out a huge sigh.

"I was so worried…"

"My poor heart…"

"Still… All things considered…"

"Yeah. I totally know what you mean."

""""That was so satisfying.""""

Someone slapped me on the behind.

I turned to see Iris looking deflated. "That was reckless, you know."

"You were cool, Branch Manager," I replied.

"Not as smooth as you. Um, I'm sorry… I'm actually feeling a bit weak from all this…"

Iris leaned on me, and I helped her to a chair.

"I'm glad you didn't lose your job," she said.

"I could say the exact same thing to you," I responded.

"G-geez…"

Someone hit me lightly on the back.

"Look at her face. The branch manager totally has the hots for him."

"They're *so* flirting…"

At that, Iris abruptly clapped her hands together.

"Okay, okay, stop dawdling. Back to work, everyone."

""""""Yes, ma'am.""""""

We returned to giving it our all for the sake of our branch manager, who apparently cared for us much more than she let on.

6
An Official Trip to the Capital, Part I

Iris had asked me to come to her office when I was free, so I did.

"What is it this time?" I asked.

"So actually... Large guilds suffer constant staff shortages... and the capital branch is the best example of that."

As Iris explained it, there seemed to be several openings in the capital. One staffer had become an adventurer, another had moved back to the countryside, and a third had gotten someone pregnant and quit after getting married. Normally, an office sought out replacements before employees left, but all these departures had been abrupt.

"So I'd like you to go to the capital's guild branch. Actually, there are several, but I'd like you to make an official business trip to the western-district one and help them out."

"You want me to aid an office in the capital?"

It wasn't as though the Lahti branch was bustling every day. There were days when adventurers would come in force, but that wasn't common.

"If you think I'm right for the task, then I will," I said, accepting.

"Thank you. That will help. You seem like you'd make up for three people in an instant." Iris pulled out a letter from her drawer. "Please give this to the branch manager there. The guild master has also been made aware of this."

"Okay, I will."

"This should be a useful learning experience for you—a chance to see how other offices function. Give it all you've got."

I was going to be away for a week. Iris informed my colleagues of the situation.

Milia looked shocked by the news "Mr. Roland i-is going to the capital...?! What if Mr. Roland...is preyed upon by a terrible woman..."

She was clearly fretting about something, but I was more likely to be the predator than the prey, so I didn't think she needed to worry.

"Roland will do the work of five people and come home in half the time, I bet."

"Do you think he'll be promoted to a branch manager...?"

"What if he runs off with a rich widow?"

Everyone offered their thoughts. Apparently there were many temptations to be had in the capital.

"Our branch was lucky enough get Roland, but we can't keep him to ourselves. Capital or not, other branches are still part of the same organization, and we should help them out. All right?" Iris said.

That got the chattering office to quiet down.

As my coworkers saw me off, they all asked me for various souvenirs.

Milia alone was looking teary-eyed as she waved a handkerchief at me. It wasn't as though I was departing for the battlefield. She was being a bit dramatic.

Since I had a Gate set up, I could come home every day, but apparently the guild I was going to help was offering to pay for my stay, so I decided to take them up on their proffered hospitality.

First, I needed to head back home to pick up some things.

"The capital...? I—I think I shall refrain from going myself...," Rila told me.

Since her last trip to the capital, Rila had been wearing her cat coin purse, which I had bought for her again, around her neck. I hadn't quite pinned down whether she had done it as a countermeasure against pickpockets or if it was a way of preventing herself from misplacing the thing. It seemed being deprived of it the first time had been traumatic.

"I will never allow that to happen again... I believe it wisest for me to avoid losing the purse you purchased for me a second time...!"

Roje had said yesterday she would be coming over tonight. So long as that elf was around, Rila wouldn't get too lonely.

"Though it is the capital, it is still work," Rila warned me. "You must put all your effort into the endeavor."

After that, Rila saw me off.

Once I arrived at the capital and got an inn room relatively close to the guild, I immediately stopped by the western district's branch.

"Oh! So you're the help they sent?"

Stan Jacka, the western branch's manager, adjusted his glasses, moving them up and down as he looked between me and the letter I had brought.

"I'm Roland Argan. I have come from the Lahti branch."

"Obviously I already know that. It's written right here." Stan patted the letter with his hand. "I'm not sure what a rookie can offer us, though." The tired-looking man let out a rather drawn-out and dramatic sigh. He appeared to be in his midforties.

"I assure you I am capable of fulfilling my duties. Please tell me what you need."

"Listen, bud, offices in the capital are nothing like those in the countryside. Understand? Just 'cause you can get the job down there doesn't mean you'll be successful here."

"I don't believe Lahti would be considered rural—"

"Compared to the capital, it is. We're not running a training school here, so I don't want to hear the words *I don't know*, *No one ever told me*, *I can't do it*, or any other possible iteration of those phrases."

Stan glanced into the office. It was much larger than the Lahti one and had ten seats at the counter, which were all occupied by a staff member working with adventurers.

"Get going," Stan instructed. "The adventurers never stop coming, so go help them. That's your job."

The man turned right around and headed to his office. Since I would be working with them for a while, I observed how everyone went about their tasks as I introduced myself to each staff member.

They were busy, of course, so the greetings were perfunctory. Still, I was able to ascertain how things operated.

In addition to those adventurers being served, there were fifty others waiting on sofas in the back—and more lined up outside.

The staffers were all clearly on edge from how busy things were.

I organized documents that had been placed on the countertops and took a reception spot, bringing the number of adventurers the guild could serve at once up to eleven.

I didn't need a chair.

Things ended quickly.

"Here, please! This way for reporting quest information! Quest reports here! Any adventurers with a quest to report, please make your way over!" I called out, earning some incredulous looks from my coworkers at first. Yet once they decided I wasn't inconveniencing them, they returned to their duties without complaint.

Adventurers sitting on the sofas came over immediately.

"I have a Rock Bat slaying quest to report on."

"I see. That's a D-rank quest with a payout of two thousand rin per bat."

"Yeah, that's right."

The Lahti branch offered the same job. There were some quests that were limited by region, but gathering and slaying quests tended to have wide-scale recruitments. They also required appraising, which took time.

"Thank you for your work. I'll check these."

There were twenty-four teeth in the jute bag the adventurer handed to me.

They all seemed to be from the monster, based on the shapes.

"Well, it seems you've slayed twelve, so—"

"Hey! There are twenty-four of them in this bag! I slayed twenty-four!"

Bang, the ornery adventurer slapped the counter in an attempt to intimidate me.

"I am counting two as one slaying. Since each one has two fangs."

"...S-seriously?" the man replied, averting his eyes.

Had he really thought acting aggressively would work? Perhaps he thought he could throw his weight around because I was new.

"Please don't try to trick the guild staff. We're the ones who arrange your quests. The guild decides who gets the difficult and better quests," I scolded.

"Uh... S-sorry... I won't try pulling that ever again..." As the adventurer shrugged and apologized in a low voice, I handed him his reward.

No sooner did he leave than another adventurer came to take his place. I appraised the herbs they turned over and presented the proper remuneration. Next was a young man, then a woman...

As I worked through the queue of quest reports, the line of waiting adventurers began to shrink.

"Huh... This is easier...than usual...?"

"Yeah... I've only been arranging quests."

"It's thanks to the specialized report counter."

When you were only working on one type of task, it was easier to repeat because you didn't have to change your focus. This made mistakes less frequent as well.

"Thanks for the help." Someone who appeared to be a veteran staff member clapped me on the shoulder.

"Don't mention it," I responded.

Once all the adventurers making reports had left, Stan came in.

"You. I caught that. You didn't send any of those items off for appraisal."

"Yes, since I was capable of inspecting them on my own."

"And where are your qualifications? I'm talking a license—a lie-sense. You haven't got one, have you?" Stan's eyes were wide as he slapped the countertop.

"I believe it was mentioned in the letter," I told him.

"What was?"

"You only read the first page and not the back," I stated.

Stan tilted his head to the side quizzically and pulled the missive from his pocket. At my prompting, he flipped the paper over.

"*Please have Roland Argan work as an appraiser during the duration of this trip.* What the—?! Who scrawled this on here?!" As Stan read aloud, his pupils shrunk to points. "Th-the guild master?"

The term *appraiser* generally applied to people who were experts in a variety of tools and materials. I was rather surprised myself when the guild master said I should be treated as one, but his signature was on the letter. Evidently, Tallow wanted to take advantage of me as much as possible. I was capable of inspecting the spoils of a quest, but his personal endorsement on that front was a bit excessive.

"You're correct in that I do not have a license," I admitted. "However, I have it in writing from the guild master to treat me as if I did. If you have complaints, please direct them to him."

"Grrr…"

"Furthermore, sending the materials to the proper posts creates more labor. There are few appraisers as it is. When one is available, it's more efficient to have them working in a specialized role," I explained.

"Th-that's no reason to make decisions all on your—"

From behind Stan, one of the appraisers spoke up. "Um, Branch Manager."

"What?"

"Well, I also checked the turn-ins…"

"And he wasn't consistent, right? This isn't a job you can rush. What are we going to do about the rewards he's already paid out?!"

"I did an additional appraisal of everything, but he was right each time."

"Huh?"

"He identified thirty-two types of materials—everything from proof of slayings to the number of herbs collected, and of those nearly two hundred items, he was never wrong."

"…"

Adventurers and guild staffers had come to watch at some point and were staring at Stan, waiting for him to respond.

"…Y-you got lucky, newbie. Today was a light day, damn it."

"Um, Branch Manager."

"What?"

"We actually had more adventurers in today. We were afraid we'd be working through until morning before he came to help."

"..."

Everyone was waiting in silence for the branch manager to say something.

"K-keep up the good work!" Stan shouted, then he returned to his office as though beating a retreat.

"Argan, have any plans tonight?" one of the staff members asked me around closing time.

"We were hoping to hold a little welcome party for you."

"I'm grateful for the thought, but I'm only going to be here for one week. It's not as though I'll stay forev—"

"Oh, c'mon, don't speak in absolutes."

Another carefree-looking coworker wrapped an arm around my shoulders.

"It's just to have a quick drink in a place with some beautiful broads, you get me?" He leaned in close.

Though I would only be here a few days, I still worked with these people, so I reasoned that getting better acquainted with them wasn't a bad idea.

"All right. Just for a bit," I said.

We closed up for the day, and I headed out on the streets with three staff members I had gotten to know that day. Apparently we weren't drinking at a wholesome establishment, as they led me to the pleasure district.

It was an area some referred to as a dump. This part of town was definitely a bit odd, and it lacked sophistication, but in a good way, which gave it its own kind of entertaining charm. We arrived at one of the district's many nightclubs. The dimly lit establishment was chock-full of gaudily dressed women serving men alcohol. The place was alive with the sound of high-pitched cheers.

An ostentatious-looking employee turned around and addressed me. "I'm sure you'll find a girl or two who'll catch your fancy, so you have fun with them."

"Uh-huh..."

It seemed the others in my group were already spellbound.

I hadn't understood the point of paying money specifically for women to serve you alcohol, so I'd never stepped foot in a place like this before. Still this was as good a chance as any to indulge in the experience.

Since it was meant to be a welcome party for me, my colleagues were paying for me anyway.

We headed into the back of the club. After waiting on a sofa for a bit, six decked-out women came by and served us. I drank in silence, while my coworkers struck up some idle chitchat with the waitresses. I didn't have anything to say to girls I didn't know. The other guild staffers' nostrils flared as they broached numerous topics, both real and false.

"You can really hold your liquor, sir. You've done nothing but drain your cup. Do you enjoy drinking?"

A woman named Feelie sat down next to me and replenished my empty glass. Then she cut it with water and mixed it for me, a tactic likely to prevent people from getting too inebriated.

"Not really," I replied.

"You're the shy type, aren't you? You can talk about whatever you'd like, even things you don't normally share."

Feelie moved close to me, placed her hand on my thigh, and looked up with puppy-dog eyes.

"..."

"Hee-hee. Are you nervous?"

Based on the conversation the others in my group were engaged in, they had called for women they already knew. They were chatting up a storm.

I see.

Men without much experience with women likely misunderstood things in situations like these.

A waiter called for Feelie, and she stood to leave me.

"I need to run over to some other customers. I hope you enjoy yourself," she purred. After a charming wink, she sauntered off, and another girl came to replace her.

I headed to the restroom and caught a glimpse of the guy who was currently with Feelie.

"Oh, Feeliiiiie..."

"My, you really shouldn't, Manager."

Feelie was seated next to Stan. It seemed he had been the one to call her over.

Do all the men at this branch office frequent this place?

Stan's nostrils were also flared, just like my other coworkers. It seemed like he might huff and puff and blow her right down with the zeal he exhaled.

Chapter 6   125

Feelie quickly evaded Stan's puckered lips. To me, it seemed an inane scene.

As Stan whispered something to the woman, he pulled her closer by the shoulders and rubbed her thigh. He was very clearly enjoying himself. The club must have been a favored place for blowing off steam from work.

Once I returned from the bathroom, I discovered that Stan was getting even more physical with Feelie.

"Please, Manager... That's too much."

"What's the problem? I always spend the big bucks on you. You wouldn't make nearly as much if not for me. Feelie, babyyyy, give me a meoooow."

It must have been true, for Feelie went quiet at Stan's words.

He reached around her shoulders to touch her chest. The hand that had been placed on top of her thigh had, at some point, wandered in between them.

Feelie scowled, clearly waiting for this to end. Such things were undoubtedly common in places like this, but I couldn't look the other way.

"Sir, this isn't a place where you do things like that," I commanded in a dark voice, which made Stan leap away from Feelie.

"Waaaaaah! I-I'm sorrrrrry!"

It seemed he either couldn't see me because of how dim it was or because he was too frightened. Ignorant of my identity, he ducked his head and cowered.

Feelie and I shared a look, and she chuckled.

"Manager," she began. "If you're too naughty, scary men will pay you a visit, all right?"

"O-okay..."

As I tried to return to my seat, Feelie grabbed me by the hand from behind.

"Thank you," she told me.

"No. I got in the way of your work. I'm sorry."

"You didn't at all!"

The woman shook her head and quickly glanced to either side, then looked for a pen and paper and wrote something out.

"I don't...do this type of thing often, but..."

Feelie shoved the scrap of paper into my hand and turned around.

"..."

I looked at the note she had written. It explained that her shift was nearly over, and she wanted to meet somewhere to offer her gratitude.

By the time I was back in my seat, my coworkers were quite nearly blackout drunk. Since I doubted we'd be able to have a good conversation like that, I let them to pay the bill and left the nightclub.

Feelie wanted to rendezvous at the corner of an alley behind the establishment. I'd decided to only wait for a short while and go back to the inn if she didn't arrive quickly, but Feelie had beaten me there.

"I thought you wouldn't show," she said.

"I never said I wouldn't."

"I suppose so. Mr. Roland, was it? You seem like you're quite the popular man."

"I'm not at all."

"I know that's a lie."

Feelie looked at me through half-open eyes before eventually snorting with laughter. She seemed an entirely different person from the one I'd met in the nightclub. The way she carried herself made her seem young. She probably was. By my estimate, she was in her late teens.

"Would you like to…g-go somewhere quiet to drink…?" she asked me in a nervous voice that suggested she was inexperienced with such things. The girl was too shy to be straightforward.

"Just for a drink," I told her.

"Y-you're…so mean…" Feelie pouted but latched right on to my arm. "When you first came into the nightclub, I gasped a little and was kind of scared."

If money had been her aim, then Stan appeared much richer than I did, and he would have been easier to weasel money out of.

I let Feelie lead the way to a cheap boardinghouse that looked as though it were about to lean over sideways. This was where she lived.

"I thought we were going to another business," I said.

In the dim light, Feelie hugged me, but I slowly pushed her back.

"Don't sell yourself short," I told her.

Nervously, Feelie managed to say, "I-I'm sorry if I made you feel awkward... I-I'll do really good..."

"Once you've grown into a woman, I'll ask for you," I replied.

I gave her a pat on the head and turned to leave.

◆

The next day, I went to work at the western branch office of the capital again.

Thanks to the split in quest arrangements and reports, things weren't as chaotic as yesterday.

"How many times are you gonna get it wrong?"

"S-sorry..."

The voices of a scowling female employee and a deflated male one tore through all others.

"You're not learning what you're supposed to do. Mistakes are forgivable *once*. You can't keep making them repeatedly."

"Yes, I'm sorry..."

From what I could tell, everyone else was used to this being a frequent occurrence. Once they saw who was involved, they went straight back to their tasks.

"All he did yesterday was organize documents, right?" I asked the woman next to me at the counter.

"Yes... Um, this is going to sound harsh, but...I understand how she feels. He keeps making the same silly errors whenever we're busy. It's pretty normal, so don't worry about it."

The male employee being scolded was named Ludo, if I recalled correctly.

"Mr. Ludo doesn't look very comfortable being here," I remarked.

"That's because he's been a burden..."

Ludo seemed to be about my age, but he was bashful and rarely spoke. There was something about him that gave off a flighty air, and he tended to look every which way, his eyes flitting about. It was reminiscent of a wild animal on alert for predators.

"..."

A line of adventurers waiting for quests had formed outside the guild.

There were many adventurers within the capital, partially because the job variety was more diverse, but it was also because the payout here was higher than in Lahti.

I quickly scribbled a couple questions on a piece of paper and handed them to Ludo, who was hunkered down in his seat.

"Excuse me, could you make several of these? They should all be the same."

"Huh? Y-you mean me?"

"Yes."

I glanced over at the woman who had chewed out Ludo. She nodded. Evidently, Ludo didn't have anything demanding at the moment.

"Please," I said.

"Uh...?"

Though Ludo seemed bewildered and tilted his head quizzically several times, he nonetheless acquiesced.

Evidently, he felt guilty for not having anything to do while our colleagues were busy, which made him worried about the looks others gave him, which left the man uncomfortable.

"I've finished, Mr. Argan," he called.

Ludo had made about a hundred copies of the questions I had written out.

"Thank you. Now, please hand these forms and some pens to the adventurers in the office and have them fill out the sheets."

"Okay...," Ludo replied vacantly as he left the counter. With pens and papers in hand, he made his way to the adventurers who were chatting idly on the sofas. "Please fill these out and bring them up with you," he requested sheepishly.

Although the adventurers gave him dubious looks, once they saw the forms, they started scribbling responses. Other staff members quickly grew curious about what was happening.

"Next person, please."

The adventurer who had been called by a staff member stood up from the sofa and handed the form to the employee.

"So...I'm supposed hand this to you, right...?"

"Huh?"

The guild staffer read over the form carefully.

"Name, age, gender, rank, type, and rank of desired quest... party experience and skill..."

I'd drafted a quick reception questionnaire, and Ludo had made copies of it.

Since we didn't have nearly as many adventurers waiting in line at the Lahti branch, asking questions orally sufficed. However, the same didn't hold true at this branch.

"We don't need to waste time on the basic inquiries anymore..."

A quest had to be arranged based on what an adventurer was looking for, and getting all the relevant information could take a while. In the meantime, adventurers queued up with nothing to do.

"How would this one be?"

"Great, I'll take it," the adventurer responded.

Quest assigning had become astonishingly smooth.

"I-it's like we've had a revolution..."

"There's a new wind blowing through the western branch today..."

Despite my coworkers' words, it didn't really feel quite that incredible to me.

"Mr. Argan, I'll make more of these!"

Ludo had undoubtedly been feeling awful for being a burden and unable to help. Now he happily seized the initiative to make more reception forms.

"What do you think you're doing?" Stan had emerged from the back, looking as grumpy as ever. "Your job is to help everyone else since they're all busy. Why're you bothering with this superfluous stuff?" He walked over, attempting to stare me down. "You've been acting as you please since you arrived. Why couldn't Iris have sent me someone more competent?"

Perhaps this was why the guild employees at this branch treated a small change like a revolt, because Stan quashed any alterations to the standard formula.

I stood and brought my face right up to his. "I've been helping just as you wanted," I answered.

"Wh-what do you think you're doing? You trying t-t-to pick a fight with me?!"

Although he was flustered, Stan balled his trembling hands into fists.

He looked like a child getting into their first scuffle.

"I'm helping someone who hasn't thought to wonder why his employees are so busy all the time," I explained.

"W-we have our way of doing things around here, you little—!"

Now it wasn't just his fists that were trembling, but his knees, too.

"I won't go as far as to say your way of doing things is incorrect. However, you're adhering to legacy methods from a time when there were fewer adventurers and quests. Please look at the situation for yourself before you pass judgment. You've had three people quit, and you need to figure out how to adapt while you're understaffed. That requires original ideas."

"Guh..."

"If you need to call for help in a time like this, that's basically another way of saying that you lack the abilities to address the issue yourself."

"Grrr..."

A male employee whispered, "That's right. The branch manager never looks at what's actually going on. All he does is hand out orders."

"Even when he knows he's missed the mark, he flies off the handle when anyone doesn't listen to him."

"Wh-who said that?! Wh-who's pointing out my flaws?!"

Stan looked around, but instead of averting their eyes, all the staffers stared right back at him. Clearly, they all felt the same way.

"They're not just pointing fingers. They're telling you how it feels being on the ground level," I stated, but Stan no longer appeared interested in listening. His face was bright red.

"Is this a revolt?! Is mutiny what you're after?! Fine by me. If you don't want to listen to what I'm telling you, then you can quit!"

"…Why don't you quit instead?"

"Huh?"

"Yeah, you only became a branch manager because of your connections."

"What?"

"We can all tell you don't actually do any work."

"Um, wait—"

"Let's write a petition to get him transferred."

"…Y-you're all screwing with me, right?"

No one answered that, but a sour mood hung over the office.

"Did you get your baby Feelie to meow for you?"

"Uh… H-how do you know about that…?"

Stan took several steps back.

"I can't believe you'd stick your hand between a girl's thighs when she clearly didn't want it…and that you used your other hand to fondle her breast at the same time."

All my female coworkers regarded Stan with disgust.

"Y-you guys, you've gotta cool your heads…," the branch manager squeaked out before retreating to his office.

At the end of the day, Stan apologized for his behavior. He spoke in a voice that was barely perceptible to the human ear, but that was enough to satisfy the employees.

"The closing time at this branch is awfully late. Is there a reason for that?" I asked Stan. We were in his office.

"That's because… Uh… There are adventurers who come in very late to make reports…"

"In that case, let's set business hours to end at nine at night and only keep a reporting counter open after that. From what I've seen, there are so few adventurers coming in after dark that I could count the number on my hands."

"R-right…"

Stan was taking notes on my advice.

We sat across from each other at a low table. It would have been tough to discern who was the real superior in this situation.

Stan had asked me for assistance on how to manage the guild branch, so I had started giving him suggestions. After apologizing during closing yesterday, he had come to the realization that he had been doing things all wrong.

"Since appraisals take time, what do you think of collecting materials that are turned in, then paying the reward the next day when the adventurer comes back to report for duty? There's only ever two or three people who come in to report on quests immediately after opening," I proposed.

"Y-you're right... The appraisers typically don't have anything to do early in the day..." Stan nodded to himself as he kept writing. "That being the case, do you think we only need one person there for reports during closing time...?"

"I think that would be most desirable. Doing so would keep employees from pointlessly staying late."

I was only giving advice. As the manager, Stan had to decide whether my ideas were good for the branch. Stan was a stubborn man, so he had been firm about upholding the rules and customary procedures all this time. Efficiency had been a secondary concern, or rather, he likely had never given it much consideration to begin with. According to his subordinates, he had connections with nobles and had been promoted to branch manager without much experience.

Evidently, friends in high places could carry one far in the Adventurers Guild.

Stan had gained his position because of who he knew, yet he had no idea how to do the work. He hadn't even asked his employees what their day-to-day operations were like. It was no wonder the people who worked under Stan resented him.

The office was a powder keg of negativity. That was why everyone had gone off on Stan the other day.

"Do you think there'll be adventurers complaining if we suddenly change the system?" Stan questioned.

"Possibly, but you can have the staff guide adventurers through the new systems while arranging quests."

"I suppose you're right." Stan suddenly stopped writing and muttered, "I wonder if...my employees will accept this."

"I'm afraid I can't answer that for you. Don't command them to obey, though; just have a conversation with them all."

After working here for a few days, I had realized that the Lahti branch functioned as a team.

"They report to you, but they're also your partners. You should bring them together so they operate in union."

"...Uh-huh."

Stan's entire attitude differed from yesterday, and he was being incredibly sincere.

"The other branches in the capital have been doing things the same way ever since I started. I think other managers might complain if I shake things up...," Stan said, concerned.

Suddenly, a guild staffer burst in, looking flustered. "Excuse me! Um! Mr. Argan... S-s-someone is here to see you!"

"Excuse me?"

"Th-th-the guild master is here!"

"Please tell him I'm not present," I replied.

"Well, but..."

"Heeey! Rolaaand! I know you're heeere! Come on ouuut!"

I heard a very familiar and loud voice from outside the office.

"Tsk."

"Did you just cluck your tongue?!"

After giving Stan a bow, I left.

In the reception room, I found a large, unshaven man with a square face standing on the other side of the counter.

"Still as loud as ever, I see," I greeted.

Tallow gave a loud laugh in response. "That's my one redeeming feature!"

"I'll have you know: I hate people who shout needlessly."

"Ha-ha-ha. Oh, don't be like that."

Just like when Tallow had summoned me to the guild headquarters, I was certain whatever he had to tell me couldn't be anything good.

"Mr. Argan is talking to him casually."

"He's even telling the guild master he doesn't like him to his face!"

"Are they friends, or do they hate each other?"

Tallow dropped himself down into one of the reception seats. When I saw him do that, I tried to shoo him away with my hands.

"You're in the way. That's where adventurers sit."

"Oh, pardon me. Sorry about that!"

I led Tallow to a meeting room, where we wouldn't bother anyone.

Tallow wasted no time collapsing into a sofa. I didn't intend for this conversation to run overlong, so I took a seat on the edge.

"So what is it? For a guild master, you appear to have a lot of free time."

"Don't be so sarcastic with me. Despite what you may think, I'm very busy."

I shrugged.

"When you stopped by the capital for a seminar, the headquarters realized we're old friends. That's why Lahti received a commendation, you see. That achievement was mostly thanks to your abilities."

"It wasn't just because of me."

"So you claim. From an objective vantage point, anyone can see that you're the one bringing in results."

"I don't care what others think," I responded.

"Look, just listen to what I've got to say. Several branch managers who are aware of Lahti's recent successes are asking for you to work at their offices."

"Did you really come here just to talk about employee poaching?"

"Do you ever lose that frigid attitude? It's not charming at all. There are even some branches that are willing to double your salary. A few higher-ups don't think you're being compensated well enough."

I had the Gate spell. No matter which branch I worked at, I wouldn't have trouble with the commute.

Tallow pulled some documents out of his breast pocket and unfurled them on the table. Because of where he had been storing them, they were moist from sweat and rather crumpled.

"I also hate it when you do that," I commented.

"Whatever could you mean?" Tallow looked at me, wide-eyed.

"Nothing." I shook my head and listened as Tallow launched into his explanation.

The papers were transfer requests from other offices. They listed where each branch was, what the salaries were, and other benefits.

"What do you think? Will you consider the offers?"

"Does Iris know about this?"

"She does, but she decided to keep out of it, since she knows how skilled you are."

"I see."

I wondered what Rila would say if I talked to her about it. Her own home life wouldn't change, so she'd probably just be happy for me.

"I'll be at the headquarters, so please stop by. If I'm not, just grab a random employee and hand off a letter to them for me." With that, Tallow rose from his seat and departed.

"I can't describe eavesdropping as a good habit to develop," I stated, prompting Stan to enter.

"Sorry. I was so curious about what the guild master wanted with you... You seem pretty amazing, Argan."

"You mean because of the headhunting?"

"Yeah! Sometimes the Adventurer Association asks branches to transfer personnel from one place to another, but this is the first time I've seen offices request a specific person!"

"Really?"

"Working your way up the ladder...getting promoted... That's what a guy's gotta do." Stan nodded enthusiastically to himself. "After all your proposals, I know you can't end your career as a run-of-the-mill employee. You're not regular-worker quality."

"I'm not regular-worker quality...," I echoed. Was that true? I'd thought I was average this whole time! Utterly shocked, I couldn't stop myself from asking, "Do you mean I'm not *normal*...?"

"Normal is whatever you decide it is. You're only here for a week to help out, but I'd like you to stay forever." Stan laughed, gave me a slap on the shoulder, and left.

7
An Official Trip to the Capital, Part II

◆Iris◆

Sitting in her office, Iris let out a groan.

It was already growing dark outside as closing time approached. Ever since she'd heard *that* from the guild master, she hadn't been able to focus on work.

"Other branches have asked about recruiting Roland. Five of them."

Though she had been surprised, it was only logical that other managers would seek to claim Roland after learning about him. Not only was the man capable at guild work and never made mistakes, but he was also an incredibly skilled combatant. He even made those working around him try harder. Someone like him was practically unheard of.

Iris had claimed she wouldn't butt into the matter in an attempt to act cool, but...

"I hope he stays...," she whispered.

"Branch Manager? We're locked up, so it's time for the closing meeting," Milia called, stepping into the branch manager's office.

"You'll probably cry when the time comes...," Iris lamented.

"What do you mean?"

Iris shook her head and stood up. "Nothing."

Once Iris reviewed the day's events and gave advice for tomorrow, the peaceful workday came to an official end.

Just as everyone went to get ready to go home, she said, "Milia, do you have anything you're doing tonight?"

"You never ask me to go out, Branch Manager... I'm free ♪," Milia answered, looking to be in high spirits. Undoubtedly, the young woman was anticipating a free meal.

Iris gave the girl a strained smile and retreated back to her own office to get ready to go home. Then she waited by the back entrance for Milia.

"Where are you taking me?"

"We're going for drinks today," Iris answered.

"Wow. You're really getting into it tonight."

At the restaurant, the two gulped down wine from fancy glasses.

"This is so nice!" Milia exclaimed.

Iris, however, looked rather deflated. "Hahhhhh..."

"Please don't sigh so loudly when we're supposed to be out enjoying ourselves!"

"You're right... I shouldn't be so down... Ugh..."

"Oh, I know what happened. Did Mr. Roland officially turn you down?"

"...You're not too far off."

"Huh? But I was only joking... How is it *almost* like that...?"

Iris emptied her glass as soon as the waiter came by to refill it. "He's so amazing, so it was bound to happen... Anyone...would... want him...even though I was the one who interviewed and hired him..."

Milia seized her sniffling boss by the shoulders.

"What is it? What's going on, Branch Manager?!"

"I thought it would be best to tell you first...just in case it does happen..."

"J-just in case *what* happens...?" Milia audibly swallowed.

"Roland might transfer to another branch."

"Whaaaaaaa—?!"

"Other offices can give him more than we can. So he might..."

"W-we need to stop him. Right, Branch Manager?"

"We can't. Don't be so selfish."

"Why not? You don't want him to leave, either."

"... You're right. But...I can't envision Roland remaining a regular employee forever..."

Now Milia was sighing, too. "So he's getting promoted?" she questioned.

"Mostly likely. I'm sure Rila will be over the moon," Iris replied. "She always dotes on him, no matter what happens."

"She really does..." After Milia had finished her win, she flagged down a waiter and requested another drink. "I want the same thing, in a stein instead of a glass, please."

"Huh? A-a stein?"

"Yes, please."

The two women picked at some food.

Tongue now loosened by alcohol, Iris continued, "I'm sure there are going to be adventurers who'll want to go with Roland."

Milia, meanwhile, glugged the drink like it was water.

"…You really can hold your liquor," Iris remarked.

"Hee-hee. Just a little."

During the get-together at Roland's house a while back, Iris had gotten the impression that Milia was a lightweight, but she must have been politely holding herself back.

"Roland is returning in two days. I'm sure the guild master will have spoken with him by then," Iris stated gloomily.

"Let's try getting Miss Prima Donna to stop it from happening."

"You're really not one to keep things bottled up, are you, Milia?"

"What's so wrong about that? If it's mature not to say what you want, then I wanna stay a kid. Let's go to Mr. Roland's house."

"Huh? You mean right now?"

"We need to strike while the iron is hot. C'mon!" Milia pressed. Iris put up little resistance, and before long, the two were off for Roland's place.

◆Roland◆

"…And that's what apparently happened, knave."

"I see."

When I'd come home to consult Rila about the recruitment

calls, I'd found Iris and Milia hopelessly drunk and splayed out on the sofa.

Their stomachs and underwear were bare for the world to see, so I couldn't look at them.

I placed a jacket over Milia to hide her white panties. Iris seemed to be wearing underwear as well, though it was difficult to tell as it didn't cover her buttocks.

"I cannot believe Iris would wear such ridiculous undergarments... It is practically all on display! Can such a thing truly be called clothing?!" Rila exclaimed, seemingly shocked.

"Take your hand off the edge of her skirt," I told her.

Once I'd pulled a blanket over Iris, I sat down at the end of the sofa.

"They came to ask me for something, it seems. However... when I opened a bottle of wine, this is what happened. They grumbled an awful lot, but in the end, they mostly just drank." Rila giggled as she sat down on my lap. She positioned herself perfectly to be cradled in my arms, just like a princess. "So what will you do? I heard the news from the two drunkards."

"What do you think about it?" I questioned.

"Hmm? I am thrilled. Clearly, your superiors have finally taken notice of your superior abilities both on and off the battlefield. This shall raise my standing as well, for I am the person who chose you."

"I see."

Rila's frank and admittedly surprising remarks left me wanting to think over the job offers a little more.

"I asked the branch manager in the capital branch I visited what a *normal* person would do. He told me I needed to decide that for myself."

"Mm-hmm. I believe he is quite right about that. Yes, mayhap you seek confirmation about what is normal from others too often."

"That's because I have no standard for it, myself."

"Can you simply not decide upon what is normal simply by how it feels?"

Now we were getting deep. And difficult.

Rila flipped over Milia's skirt from under the jacket I had laid on her. "So plain," she remarked.

"Please don't ogle someone's panties right after impressing me."

"...So what do you think? Be honest," Rila pressed.

Suddenly, Iris pulled herself up. Her eyes were still unfocused, and her face was still red. "Roland, don't... Yer one of mine... So you cwan't... You cwan't... I don't want you to go somewhere else..."

Having made her case, she promptly collapsed again and was sound asleep in moments.

Next Milia woke up. "Ugh... I feel terrible... My head hurts..."

"Would you like to go to the bathroom?"

"Huhhh... Is that you, Raland...? Meester Raland, yer right in fwont of my eyes..." After laughing, Milia's expression suddenly turned serious, then she flopped right back over onto her side. "Meester Raland... If you're gone, I'll cwy... Wah-waaaaaaah..."

Fat tears streamed down Milia's cheeks.

"It seems they love you very much, knave. Or shall I say Meester Raland?"

"She's just slurring her words."

Rila kissed me as Milia sobbed beside us.

"I still had not given you your welcome-home kiss."

"Was now really the best time for that?"

"*I—I shall tell you again… I do not care who you bequeath your seed to… However…that does not mean that I am immune to jealousy…*"

Embarrassed, Rila kept her volume only slightly above a mumble. I caressed her cheek, stroking it several times.

"Hmm… How do I feel…?" I wondered aloud.

Since we hadn't seen each other for several days, Rila refused to let go. Once morning came around, the other two were groaning from hangovers as I headed back to the western branch in the capital.

◆

When my weeklong business trip was over, I enjoyed a two-day break, and after that, I would finally return to my duties at the Lahti branch.

"Seems like you were a big help over there," Iris stated. I was in her office reporting on what had happened. "'*We were wasting our personnel and their time, but Argan made sure we were soon hard at work,*' according to Stan. Nice job."

Iris undoubtedly was acting formal because of that matter with the guild master.

"So about the recruitment calls from the other branches," I began.

"Huh? Uh, oh, sure..." At first, Iris's shoulders twitched, but then she quickly settled herself.

"I turned them all down. I look forward to continuing to work with you."

"Huh? Are you sure about that...?"

"Yes."

This time, I'd made my decision not based on what others considered normal, but what felt right for me.

"Wh-what a relief... I need to tell Milia—"

Iris quickly scampered out of the room like a young girl.

A better job meant a greater salary, which would lead to a more outlandish lifestyle. However, Iris, Milia, and all my other coworkers wouldn't be part of it. Surely, the fact that I wasn't especially greedy played a part in my choice, too. More money didn't spark any interest in me.

"It seems I've grown accustomed to this place without even realizing it," I whispered to myself with a little smile.

8
A Broadscale Quest and a Former Companion, Part I

Iris entered the office with documents in her hands. "Do you have a minute?"

"Yes, we've just finished handling the adventurers," I replied.

Some very earnest adventurers had come into the guild this morning. Fortunately, I'd already set them up with a quest and seen them off. There weren't too many other adventurers in the guild at the moment.

"We've received a broadscale quest from the guild master." Iris set several sheets on my desk. "The client is the Adventurer Association. It's been a while since we've had a big undertaking like this in our region."

I read over the documents. A subterranean cave had recently been discovered in the area, and the Adventurer Association wanted to conduct an investigation.

"A subterranean cave... Should the guild really be taking the initiative on exploring this?" I asked.

When traipsing into unexplored areas, it was likely one would run into rare vegetation, wildlife, monsters, and beasts. Although perilous, it was possible to discover rare valuables in such locales.

Thus, uncharted places were considered high risk, high reward. There was a chance some who ventured out to the cavern wouldn't return alive.

When I read more closely, the tip had come from an adventurer, and he had been paid for his information.

"Seems the one who found the cave chose a no-risk but easy payout instead of exploring the place for a better profit."

"I guess so," Iris agreed.

Iris motioned for me to follow her to her office. "Let's discuss the details in private," she said.

I did as requested.

"So. The guild master, Tallow, has asked for you to take charge of this quest as the tactical adviser," Iris explained.

"Is that right?" I had no idea what to do, but apparently the Adventurer Association and the guild headquarters were entrusting the whole operation to me. "...Is that a polite way of saying they're pushing the work onto me?"

"I wouldn't go that far. They simply trust you as the tactical adviser. You should be honored. I want you to prioritize this. I'm going to take you off of normal duties. Please give this your undivided attention."

"I will."

I brought the documents with me back to my seat. No one knew how much power it would take to excavate the uncharted cavern. That fell into the realm of surveying.

I looked through our register of adventurer names.

"It isn't a true survey unless they make it back alive to give a report..."

Though there was no limit to how many people could be involved in a broadscale quest, they were still heading into the unknown. We didn't know how spacious the path would be, so it would be dangerous to send a large crowd. In the worst-case scenario, those bringing up the rear could obstruct people in the front from trying to retreat. When I considered that, it seemed best to only deploy a small group.

Milia must have heard me talking to myself, because she came over and asked, "Mr. Roland, you've been mumbling to yourself for a while now. Is something wrong?"

"A broadscale quest was announced, and as the tactical adviser, I've been tasked with leading it."

"I heard you'd become the tactical adviser, but...what do you actually do as one?"

"The Adventurers Guild wants an employee holding the reins instead of an adventurer in large-scale operations."

"That's amazing! So the guild master picked you out of every possible employee! Mr. Roland, you're incredible!" Milia innocently clapped.

Our female coworkers' ears perked up, but they otherwise didn't react.

"The guild master has formally acknowledged Mr. Argan's skills...?"

"Which means...he's on the fast-track for a promotion..."

"He could end up the youngest employee to be promoted to branch manager...!"

"Argan might wind up working at the headquarters... If we play our cards right, this may be a once-in-a-lifetime opportunity to live the good life in the capital."

"Sorry, Milia, but no woman could let this opportunity pass her by...!"

I could feel their eyes on me, as well as something not entirely unlike bloodlust. Milia was the only person genuinely simply happy for me.

"Were you flipping through the adventurer roster looking for who to send?" she questioned.

"Yes, but I've been having trouble selecting people."

The tactical adviser would request a suitable reward after fulfilling their duties, and that would be distributed to the adventurers once the mission was complete. First, I'd have to decide on a rank for the cavern based on how dangerous it was. Remuneration would be calculated depending on that. The first trip would just be to scout. I thought having a few veterans and some knowledgeable adventurers come along would be best, but I doubted they'd be interested in risking their necks.

"Roland, I know the perfect adventurer!" a male employee called.

"There's an adventurer I've been watching over who'd have the skills to do it," added another.

It seemed the female employees hadn't been the only ones eavesdropping.

"Thank you. I'm hoping to make a list, so—"

"I can do that for you," someone interrupted.

"No, you're not meticulous enough for that," the staffer next to them argued.

"You can't let tactless men do that. Let me," asserted a third.

I couldn't tell whether they were trying to help me or hoping to make sure I'd owe them later. I was grateful, regardless, as I'd had no idea where to start.

"Hey, c'mon, stop trying to cozy up to one of the junior employees. Haven't you guys got any shame? Geez. Finish up your own work first. Got it?" That was Maurey, acting just like his usual self. Although I didn't care for his phrasing, he was right. "You can leave it up to him. Roland's got to take full responsibility on this. Our job is to keep things running like usual."

While Maurey made some good points, his condescending demeanor robbed his words of all persuasiveness.

"Sure, Mr. Roland was tasked with the work, and we have nothing to do with it, but…as fellow coworkers, shouldn't we pitch in? Mr. Roland always helps us, and I'm sure this is a large task for one person…"

Several of the staff members who had been bickering with each other went quiet once Milia chimed in.

"…I suppose you're right."

"Being a tactical adviser must be tough!"

"Let's start by deciding when the exploration is going to begin, shall we?"

Everyone who'd been listening suddenly offered to lend a hand.

"There's a really tight-knit group of adventurers who should return from a quest in five days. Depending on how they feel, we might be able to start in seven days. What do you think?"

"Thank you. Since you're helping me with choosing people, then I think we can set the start date for seven days from now," I said, which prompted a more senior colleague to reply, "Everyone, let's make a list of adventurers who would take on a quest like this."

"That means anyone who will be available in a week! And don't forget to write down their skill if you know it!"

"And they've got to be real team players!"

After someone mentioned that, everyone laughed. There were a lot of solo adventurers who just couldn't work in groups, even though they were skilled.

"What will we do about water, food, and supplies?"

"Apparently we can submit any expenses to the headquarters afterward."

"Someone order stuff from the secondhand shop!"

While we all went about our work, a certain man swiveled around in his seat.

"What about me? I'm one of the most experienced guys here. Want me to pitch in for my junior colleagues? Milia, babe! Need anything I could help with? Don't be shy," Maurey said as he adopted a suave pose and pointed at himself with his thumb.

"I can't think of anything, so you can focus on your own work," Milia replied.

"...Okay."

Maurey and I looked at each other.

I wished he wouldn't look so left out.

Swivel...

Maurey turned in his chair again to face away from everyone.

We compiled a list of about forty adventurers, ranked from E to A. Everyone suggested adventurers they knew well. Their skills, individual characteristics, and personalities were all described in detail.

There were all sorts of people, from those who were masters at their singular trade, to others who were knowledgeable about many things, to talented people who were low ranked but capable nonetheless.

"Thank you so very much, everyone," I stated. "This will be a big help."

"Don't mention it. Make sure to speak up if you ever need assistance, yeah?" Maurey responded with a smug look on his face.

A staff member who had gone out earlier returned and informed me that they had procured water, travel rations, and recovery potions for the broadscale quest.

"Don't be afraid to lean on us a little."

"Yeah, since you're always the one helping us, Roland."

I thanked everyone again.

After checking on the provisions, I took the list we had created and got to work picking out members for the special party. Ultimately, this would still be a survey job. We required people who could fight, but there would likely be other needs as well.

A few days later, I was making my best attempt at soliciting people to join the expedition group.

Even when I was able to find adventurers from the list and explained the situation, they regarded me doubtfully as they shook their heads. Not knowing the exact danger or reward was dissuading to an adventurer.

I could have gone on my own, but that would mean denying others prestige and money.

That wouldn't look good for the guild, either. There'd be no need for adventurers if staffers could handle everything, after all.

As I crossed off yet another name on my list, Dey entered the office.

"Oh, Master Roland, I've finished my quest."

"...Bingo. How very convenient."

Through some inscrutable twist of logic, becoming undead meant Dey no longer suffered under the sun, yet she was still a vampire. The darkness of a cavern was where her natural predispositions would shine. Plus, she was already dead and a skilled vanguard.

"Oh stop, did you just call me a convenient woman...? You have no idea how happy I am..."

I elected to bring along the ecstatic undead vampire with me. Truthfully, Dey was already on board before I'd even explained anything to her. She was capable enough to handle any risks, so it wasn't surprising that she had no qualms about the job.

If only there were others like her around...

When I arrived back home, I found that Roje was visiting.

"You're late, human! I suppose I shall start by congratulating you for a job well done today. Lord Rileyla made dinner and has been waiting for you."

"There we go," I said. "Someone who doesn't care about risk and can fight in the front or rear as needed. And since you're not an adventurer, you wouldn't need a reward."

"What are you blathering on about?"

I outlined things during dinner.

Roje snorted contemptuously. "Only Lord Rileyla alone may make use of me. I decline!"

Rila, who had been absentmindedly listening in, offered, "Mm-hmm, so that is what is happening. In that case, Roje, please lend him a hand."

"In that case, I, Roje Sandsong, shall accompany you!!"

With that, I now had an inanely loyal elf for my excursion.

◆

Three days later, Roje, Dey, and I gathered in front of my house.

In the intervening time, I'd tried advertising that two beautiful women were in the group in the hopes that it might attract some more volunteers, but it proved a fruitless effort.

Neal and Roger were both on a long quest and away from town.

"Hey, you, I'm only helping out because it was Lord Rileyla's command. Don't think I'm going to let you boss me around. I'm only going to fight when I want to. Got that? Well…I suppose if you beg me to save you, I might." Roje thrust her chin up haughtily as she chuckled to herself.

"Dey will be the vanguard, and I'll handle everything else. Since you haven't committed, we might not even need you," I replied.

"Wha…? But I was told to help; what do I do now…?" Roje questioned.

"You said you'd only act if you felt like it, right?"

"If I don't help you, then that's the same as turning my back on one of Lord Rileyla's edicts…! And that would be a problem…"

Roje had apparently assumed I would have to eventually beg her for assistance.

"You'll be our general combatant. There aren't many who have the talent to act both up close and far back," I told her.

"Ha, heh-heh-heh—that's right, that's exactly right! You can rely on me!"

I felt like I'd gotten better at handling Roje. Truthfully, Dey and I had the front and rear handled, so we wouldn't need a general combatant.

I distributed the bags my colleagues had prepared for us.

"These contain water, portable provisions, and other supplies like rope and such. Make sure to check what's in there. Also, if you have time, chart our route in the cave. We've included paper and a pen for that."

I planned to set up a Gate later, so if we didn't have enough supplies, we could return to the guild without issue.

"Kn-knave... Y-you..." Rila, who had snuck out through the door, handed me a flat box wrapped in a handkerchief. "'T-tis a lunch... G-good luck at work...!" she stammered, obviously incredibly bashful, then she immediately retreated back into the house.

"L-Lord Rileyla i-is so cute... The cutest person ever..." Roje marveled at this as blood ran from her nose.

Dey put on her pack and pressed us to leave the town behind.

According to the map, the entrance to the cavern was somewhere to the northwest of Lahti. Why exactly it had suddenly appeared was unclear, but it wasn't out of the question that a magical apparatus had come undone and opened a chamber previously hidden. If that was the case, it raised the question of why someone had sealed the place with magic.

We arrived at a spot that seemed to fit the bill and discovered a set of stairs mostly buried under dirt. There were also unnatural piles of earth here and there.

"I sense the vestiges of magic. It doesn't seem like the barrier was undone so much as that it lost its potency and ruptured, sending everything flying," I remarked.

The steps led us into the subterranean cavern. What looked a lot like the wreckage of what had once been a door was strewn about the ground. It seemed that this hollow had been formed through unnatural means.

There was only enough space in the passage for two to walk side by side, and the ceiling stopped at around two meters. It was likely we'd hit our heads in some sections of the cave.

Although about half a month had passed since this place was discovered, it didn't seem like anyone else had dared to explore it.

I looked at Dey. She nodded, then headed in first.

"I really do feel most at home in dark places," she stated.

Next, Roje headed in, while I took up the rear. We had lanterns prepared and illuminated the way using the flame magic Match.

The scent of damp mold filled my nostrils. Despite the construction seeming ancient, the stone path proved easy to traverse, and I didn't sense any monsters.

Roje glanced around. "What is this place?"

"That's what we've come here to find out," I responded.

"I know that," she replied.

"There's a thick layer of dust. This cavern must have been sealed off a long time ago," Dey said.

I'd thought it would be an underground maze, but it seemed that the cavern had been shaped by human hands. We didn't get lost, but we did take breaks every once in a while, and I ate the lunch that Rila had prepared for me. During those breaks, we mapped out the area.

Dey and Roje watched as I drew the chart.

"My oh my. Master Roland, it's so...adorable?"

"Ha-ha-ha. What is that thing...? Heh-heh."

The two of them giggled when they saw what I was making.

"It's easy enough to read. That's all that matters," I responded.

I took another look at the map I had made. I thought it served our needs well enough.

Roje, however, redrew it.

"Oh, very good," Dey praised. "It's very easy to read."

"Of course it is. Now do you see the difference between us, human? Ha-ha-ha!"

Honestly, hers didn't look too different...

"Then I'll leaving the charting to you, Roje."

"I suppose I have little choice then! You can rely on me!" Roje seemed energetic now that she had a task all her own. I thought she seemed rather like a dog.

We continued deeper until happening upon an old door. It was sealed through human magic, but I could easily open it by using Dispell. Beyond, we came to stop before a long stairway leading down. Glowing blue gems were set into the wall at measured intervals, so the steps were bathed in azure light.

There were benches on either side of the stairs, suggesting people were meant to sit there. The seats themselves were placed rather high up, and they silently overlooked a spacious area below.

"Round benches and a plaza down below... Perhaps this used to be an auditorium...?" I posited.

"The air here is thick with blood," Dey commented.

All along the walls were spots where the stone had been chipped or scratched. Dark crimson stained a few of the stones.

Rubbing my chin, I said, "An arena, then?"

There were no signs of life, but there wasn't dust on the seats, suggesting regular use. Suddenly we detected another presence and hid ourselves.

"There must be a second entrance," I remarked.

Roje nodded. "It seems so. In which case, the place we entered must have been…"

"It was probably an emergency exit or something," Dey finished.

While we watched from a safe place, more and more people filtered in until at least several hundred were present. They all seemed to be from the upper class. I could tell they were either nobles or affluent merchants.

Blending in as best we could, we took seats.

"*I am terribly sorry for the delay. We have finished taking your votes and have adjusted the odds slightly*," came the sonorous voice of the man evidently leading this operation as script began to appear on the arena floor.

It seemed the show did not simply consist of spectating a fight, but also placing wagers on the outcome. The names of those who would be in the next match as well as the numbers representing their odds formed on the ground. Today the schedule included one-versus-one battles as well as free-for-alls.

"*I hope you enjoy the slave-hunting opener and the main event—mortal combat.*"

Light flooded the arena as boys and girls branded with numbers from one to ten emerged. They were all young children.

Immediately, the audience grew heated. People started to shout the names of those they were betting on.

"Number Six, show me what you've got!"

"Number Two! You better hold out until you're third place or above!"

"Ha-ha-ha-ha, Number Nine's weeping!"

A half-naked, muscular man appeared. He held a hatchet in one hand and a curved cleaver in the other. The spectators burst into cheers upon his arrival.

Simply put, they were playing tag. The only differences were that those who were caught would be slaughtered and that there were onlookers—and also that there was nowhere safe to run.

"I can't think of any hobby more disgusting... How could they do this to other members of their own species?" Roje spat.

"This is why humans are the inferior species," Dey said.

Displeasure was plain on their faces.

"It likely wouldn't take us more than ten minutes to kill everyone in here," Roje stated.

"Wait." I caught her by the hand as she tried to stand, and I sat her back down.

"Why do you stop me?!"

"It might work once, but just think of the scale of this place. If we don't catch the people behind this, it will all just happen again."

Obviously, I wanted to do something, too, but we needed to find a more permanent solution. Since there were aristocrats in the audience, that meant the host also had to be a high-ranking member of society.

"And if the three of us do anything, we'll cause a commotion," I added.

However, if I was the only one to act...

Number Seven, a girl who had been racing away, was caught.

"Nooo! Stooooooop!"

People in the audience laughed as they watched the child wail and sob for her life. It was absolutely disgusting.

I leaped down the stairs and activated my Unobtrusive skill. In order to keep myself from being noticed, I moved as swiftly as possible.

"Gya-ha-ha-ha-ha!" The man in the arena grinned and let out a laugh that made me question his intelligence. He tried to bring his cleaver down on the girl.

Please, let me reach her in time.

I jumped from the audience seating and into the arena, stealing the hatchet from the large man's grip.

"Wha—? Where ax?" he said.

My eyes met the sobbing girl's. I motioned for her to keep quiet by putting my finger to my lips.

I brought down the hatchet on the man with all my might.

Shwunk.

His head went sailing into the air.

I immediately leaped away from his corpse. My skill's effects had expired, but fortunately, there was one spot the audience couldn't see. As far as I could tell, it was an exit. I hurried toward it, hiding myself in the dark. No sooner had I done so than the entire chamber erupted into an uproar.

"Wh-what just happened?!"

"Where'd his head go?"

"Ha-ha-ha! The guy died—now, that's entertainment!"

Some particularly twisted spectators believed that this development was part of the show.

Number Seven, the little girl who had been the one person to see me, came running over. The other nine kids desperately followed after.

"Uh, um... Thank you...for saving me."

"I haven't rescued you yet," I told her.

A hard kick was all it took to knock open the locked door, and we headed out of the arena. The area was deserted; there weren't even guards stationed. All ten children wore brands of servitude on their necks. Humans with too much time and money never came up with good ideas when left to their own devices.

"We'll leave this way."

Based on how this network of caverns and tunnels was laid out, I knew we could head back to the passage Roje, Dey, and I had come from. We encountered a few guards, but I knocked them out easily and brought the children back aboveground.

I was suddenly reminded of when I had rescued the pretty girl squad a while back. When asked if they had anywhere to go, all the kids shook their heads. Leaving them on their own here wouldn't help, so I established a Gate and had them jump with me back to my house.

It was my first time transporting so many people, so the effects left me exhausted. As I caught my breath at the door, Rila came outside upon hearing the commotion.

"Knave...what do you think you are doing? Did you not go to work...? And what are these children doing here?"

"I'll fill you in later. They're former slaves. Please look after them until I get back."

I'd need to undo their brands, but that had to wait. The arena was sure to be in chaos now, and I had to get back.

"Mm-hmm. All right," Rila agreed.

"I'm counting on you," I said.

The children looked hesitant, but when Rila motioned for them to come in, they entered with her.

I immediately went back to the underground arena's entrance through the Gate.

Since what Roje, Dey, and I had entered through was a sealed emergency exit, it was possible only those managing the operation knew of its existence. In which case, it was likely that they hadn't made the arena but had instead reused something that had already been created. I headed back to the audience seats and found the disarray had settled down and things were moving into the one-on-one death matches.

"I see you stole the show," Roje stated bitterly.

It seemed she had spotted me after the decapitation. Garnering attention did weaken the effects of my skill, after all.

"I don't mind a match someone has consented to, but I couldn't stand by and watch children die," I answered. "What's happening now?"

"The management apologized for the inconvenience. Now they're moving on to proper bouts," Dey explained.

"If you'd told me what you were going to do, I could've assisted...," Roje grumbled. Evidently, she carried a stronger sense of moral justice than I had expected.

"Sorry. It was easier to operate on my own with a crowd watching."

Even then, I'd only barely made it. There hadn't been time to communicate."

"It was showy, merciless, and as ruthless as lightning. What a beautiful murder," Dey commented. "I didn't get a proper look at you, but I understood it was your handiwork immediately, Master Roland." Dey giggled, looking quite satisfied.

It seemed the slave-hunting show had been the only unreasonable event. The current battle was between two armed combatants, and it became apparent quickly that nothing was off-limits. While fighters sometimes killed each other, there were other battles that ended when one side could no longer continue.

"We went and asked the people around us some questions while you were gone," Dey said.

"What did you find?"

Roje answered for her, "As far as I was able to suss out, no one knows who hosts the spectacle. They are simply invited here and attend. They say the same of the people who introduced them to this."

"I expected this to be an exclusive club that denied all outsiders, but I guess that's not the case," I replied.

None knew the identity of the ringleader, but they didn't seem to care as long as they could watch a brutal display and make their wagers. That was all these people cared about.

"It was the same for me," Dey added. "No one knew anything."

"The leader must be very thorough."

Pensively, Roje offered, "You could say that they *need* to be, given the sort of show they're running."

I nodded in agreement. It was highly probable that was the case.

For a moment, I considered taking guards prisoner for information but decided it was unlikely they'd know anything. Any who knew the truth were likely on the other side of the arena's main entrance.

Just as I tried to stand up, an announcement came on.

"And we're heading right into the next match! It's time for what you've all been waiting for! The killer of three hundred monsters and demons during the Human-Fiend War! Mercedeeeeees!"

A giant man shouldering a sword as large as an ordinary person stepped into view, and the crowd went wild.

"Mercedes! Kill 'em!"

"I've bet a million on you! I'll never let you live it down if you lose!"

"This next match will be her first mortal combat round, but please give a welcome to the self-proclaimed Masked Mage Girl!"

The whole place stirred when they saw who had entered.

It was a slender, petite young woman who kept her face concealed. She didn't look older than her early teens.

"She's just a kid!"

"C'mon, you tryin' to make a mockery of Mercedes?!"

The girl looked hesitant, but she bowed her head.

"They've let a child volunteer..." Roje's face twisted in anger.

The fight began without so much as a signal—not even a gong. Mercedes thrust his massive blade at the girl, but she was quicker on the draw, casting a spell.

"That's—," I muttered.

"Hmm... That child seems to know what she's doing."

Roje had apparently reevaluated her opinion of the Masked Mage Girl.

With a loud strumming sound, the young woman fired something resembling a magic arrow that struck her opponent dead-on. However, it didn't seem to do much damage.

"It's a bad idea to use strong magic from the start."

"Why's that?"

The girl was quick to go into action, and she began to loose weak magical attacks at the man in rapid succession.

Boos and hisses sounded from every corner of the arena.

Whenever it detected a surge of mana, an anti-magic barrier around the spectators expanded.

"You have to measure the opponent's abilities. Sure, you'll be fine if a powerful attack strikes true, but what if you miss. If they close in on you, you'll be done for immediately."

"...You're so smart, Roland..."

The Masked Mage Girl kept up her volley, but the man defended himself without much trouble.

Then a bluish-purple magic circle spread beneath the young woman's feet.

"Measure your enemy's physical capabilities with small spells, then look for an opening. Stop him in his tracks. When you know you'll hit him for sure, use the magic you're best at."

"...Got it... I'll try."

It only took the man five seconds to realize that the barrage had stopped and approach her as he maintained his guard.

This was the deciding moment.

"She has so much mana...it's terrifying... Especially considering how young she is...," Dey whispered.

When faced with an unfamiliar opponent, the way to deal with them was by keeping them diverted with quick strikes at first. Once you created an opening, you could hit them with some offensive magic that packed a punch. In the past, I instructed an eight-year-old magical prodigy on the finer points of using spells in combat. She was so capable that she'd joined the party of heroes despite her age.

"Star Blast!"

An ultramarine-colored offensive spell I had seen countless times shot out with an explosive sound.

I remembered that magic having taken down an enemy army of several thousand in the past. Fortunately, I could also tell that this particular shot hadn't been at full power.

A terrific roar tore through the arena, echoing as the audience seats shook, and their occupants shrieked. Part of the barrier meant to protect onlookers was destroyed. The man, who had been right in the direct line of the blast, had been wiped out of existence, longsword and all.

"I knew it. It's Lina," I stated.

Why my old companion was here was anyone's guess. If Almelia or Elvie knew this was the sort of thing she'd been up to, I'm sure they would have mentioned it to me.

"...That magic. I feel as though I've seen it before," Roje whispered.

The masked girl, Lina, bowed and left. What had led her to get involved in this?

"I believe she's one of my former associates," I said. "Perhaps you recognize her as the primary offensive caster from the party of heroes," I replied.

"Well, that explains it."

"I've run into her several times on the battlefield," Dey added. "I can't believe such a little girl was casting all those nasty spells... There truly are all sorts of people in the world."

If Lina was involved in this underground fighting, then perhaps she knew more about the people pulling the strings.

The main event was beginning soon, but I stood from my seat. Passages from the arena were under stricter watch than before, likely because I had taken out some guards. However, the increased security may not have been solely my doing.

There was enough room to allow two people to pass by each other in the corridors, and before long, two men who looked like enforcers for this establishment came my way.

I could have knocked them out, but I didn't want to cause more commotion.

Plus, if I couldn't slip by a pair of measly guards, I never would have survived this long.

I activated Unobtrusive, then pulled a scrap of paper from my pocket—notes from work. I hurled away from where I was and made sure it made a faint noise on impact.

"That sound just now…"

"Is something wrong?"

As the guards moved to inspect my diversion, I slipped past them.

"Guess it was just my imagination."

"Come on. Don't scare me like that."

Once they were gone, I leaped up to the ceiling. I cloaked my fingers in mana and gripped the wall. Then I silently crawled along the roof of the cavern, heading forward.

I dropped back down into the ground once in a deserted spot. Since I knew Lina was here, all I needed to do was follow her familiar mana trail.

After walking for a while, I found several rooms branching off the corridor, along with signs of monsters and magical beasts.

Undoubtedly, they were being held for shows where they would fight human slaves. I sensed Lina's presence from a door in the back. Pressing my ear close, I listened for sound in the room beyond.

"Lina, babyyy, good job out there."

The voice itself sounded male, but the tone felt feminine.

"You did great. I can give you your cut as a reward right away."

"...I'm glad... But...I feel bad...for the man I fought..."

"No, no, my dear, you shouldn't. They're all felons, so dealing with them this way is actually much better for the world."

None of the matches I'd witnessed had mentioned anything about participants being criminals. Had that been the case, the announcer likely would have explained how wicked the fighters were and listed their misdeeds to rile up the crowd.

"...If he was... I'm glad... Since I felt sorry for him..."

"My, aren't you the kind one, Lina."

"How many more times do I need to punish them, sir...?"

"Only a few more, so keep up the good work. We'll hold the next event in three days. I'll come get you. In the meantime, you can just wait."

I detected someone moving toward the door, so I faded into the shadows. No sooner had I done so than a brawny man emerged.

"..."

From his appearance, I could tell he was skilled. This was the likely the person with that sickly sweet voice.

After ensuring only one person was left in that chamber where I'd overheard the conversation, I nudged the door open slightly and peered in. The interior was decorated like a waiting room, though only sparsely. I slipped inside and shut the door behind me.

"Lina," I called.

It had been a long time since we had seen each other.

"...Roland? Roland!" The girl ran over and embraced me without asking a thing. "Roland, Roland, Roland. It's really you..."

"Everyone seems to say that whenever I reunite with them." I tried to hug Lina back, but just as I did, she latched on to my neck.

Her voice a whisper, Lina said, "I thought I'd never see you again..."

I comforted her by patting her on the head. "Looks like you've grown a little."

"Uh-huh, I did. A bit."

There were lots of things to talk about, but we were surrounded by enemies here.

"Let's catch up and talk about what's happened later. I know a route out of here. We should leave."

The person who had been speaking with Lina was clearly involved with the underground arena. He could return at any moment, too.

"Oh... Okay..."

Lina wrote a note using a pen and a sheet of paper from a nearby table. It explained that she was going out and would be back later.

One she had scrawled the crude message, she turned to me and gave a nod. Then she hurried back to my side and squeezed my hand.

"You're not...leaving again...?"

"I'm not quite sure yet," I told her.

"Hmph... You're like my elder brother...so you've got to stay with me..."

I gave Lina another pat on the head as she sulked, then we left together.

Lina carried the equivalent of a backstage pass. Anyone who saw it made no attempts to stop us as we returned to the audience seating. I'd have to figure out how the guests were coming into this underground arena later.

More importantly, I needed to report back on the mission and ask Lina what was going on.

After finding Roje and Dey, we exited through the emergency egress we had come through. Lina gripped my hand all the while and showed no sign of ever releasing it.

Dey looked the mage girl up and down. "A little runt like you did all that..."

Lina was still shy around strangers and thus stood behind me.

"What are you talking about? Magical genius doesn't depend on age," Roje stated. "That there are those who are talented with spells only a few years after their birth is just a part of the magical world."

"I know, but...her level of ability is truly absurd," Dey responded before letting out a small sigh.

Since I had used up quite a bit of my mana, I had Roje activate the Gate to bring us back to my home.

◆

Upon catching sight of Lina, Rila's eyes went wide.

"A-another child?"

"I-I'm...Lina... I-it's vewy...very nice to meet you..."

Although she slurred her words, the three women found that heartwarming.

"This seems to be tickling my budding motherly instincts..."

"M-much agreed. I feel like I'm looking at a puppy..."

"You're right. I think she needs protecting..."

Lina cowered beneath the trio's gazes and hid behind me again.

"Please stop staring as though she were an exotic animal. I will give a direct report to Iris about what has happened. This should probably go to someone higher up, but I believe the correct course of action is to inform my direct superior."

The former slave children were either bathing or eating. I removed the brand of servitude on each of them one at a time.

"Hey, human. What do you intend to do with those kids?"

"They can take the adventurer exam if they want to, or I can send them back to their hometowns, if they prefer. It will take time and effort. Roje, Rila, can I count on you to ask them what they'd like?"

"Hmph! Why would I do that—?"

"If that is what you desire, then I shall," Rila answered.

"Please leave the matter to me!"

Roje was flip-flopping again.

"Dey, please check whether there's work to be had for these children. Regardless of what they choose, they will need some money."

"Okaaay."

Rila and Roje started talking to the kids while Dey headed to the Adventurers Guild. Lina and I were left on our own.

"Well then, looks like we have a lot to talk about."

"...Uh-huh."

I sat down at the empty dining table, and Lina hopped onto my lap.

"..."

"..."

I should've known she'd do that. There was no real issue with it, however.

I quickly apprised Lina of what had transpired since we'd parted ways, omitting the bit about the demon lord.

"You...work at the guild...?"

"Yes. At the moment."

"That's so weird." Lina giggled. She was close to Maylee's age but acted a lot younger. When I asked about what had happened to her, she began to explain. "His Royal Highness...gave me lots of money, so then the orphanage I came from got lots of money, too."

Orphanages were often managed by the lords ruling over the area as part of their charity work. The director of Lina's was originally a former minister appointed by the previous lord. However, she explained that when power changed hands, things had apparently gone downhill. The newly installed lord pocketed the budget given to him by King Randolf.

He also stole all the funds Lina gave to the director (whom she referred to as her father) in order to pay off debts.

"Father said I worked really hard and didn't need to do any more, but no money ever came. He thought that was strange, so he went to ask about it…"

Ultimately, the orphanage director was arrested on charges of attempted extortion of the ruling lord.

Lina wiped tears from her eyes with her tiny hands. She would have been best off asking for help from an adult like me or someone else, but no one had been around to help her.

"Then a man named Paska came and told me, '*You need lots of money to save your father. I'll show you how.*'"

That was the man Lina had been speaking with in the underground cavern.

Somehow, he'd heard about the talented young mage. Based on his timely offering of aid, he had to have some connection to the corrupt noble. Paska had apparently only brought Lina to the subterranean arena for the first time today.

"If I fight lots and win, then he said they would let Father out of prison…"

There was no disputing that Lina was a magical prodigy, but she was still a child. Wicked people had duped her into fighting for money.

"I'm working really hard," the girl added.

"I see," I said as I gave her a pat on the head.

"…I like it when you do that…"

Lina happily pushed up into my hand. She started to get clingy and latched on to me.

We stayed like that for a bit until she fell asleep with a peaceful look on her face.

Lina had been giving it her best effort despite being all alone without anyone to consult. The more I considered how she must have felt, the greater a cold and quiet sensation grew in my chest.

"Paska, was it...?"

I had only seen him once, but I remembered his face.

9

A Broadscale Quest and a Former Companion, Part II

Milia, who'd somehow caught wind of the recent events, came by the house after work.

"Miss Milia, what's happened?" I inquired.

"Isn't it obvious, Mr. Roland?"

She held two handbaskets filled with ingredients.

"I heard you have kids in a precarious situation... You would have a mess on your hands with Miss Prima Donna's poison cooking."

Milia was practically burning with purpose.

She had been teaching Rila to cook, but they'd only had a few lessons; the former demon lord was apparently still far from up to snuff in Milia's eyes.

I took Milia's things and brought them to the kitchen.

That's when Rila popped in and asked, "Is aught amiss?"

"Miss Prima Donna, please help me. I, Milia McGuffin, will teach you some more about cooking again while you do...!"

"I doubt that will be of any use... The knave hardly seems bothered by my cooking..."

"I'm going to be very honest. Mr. Roland can only stomach that stuff because he's abnormal."

M-me? Not normal...?

"Roland looks rather upset by that remark," Roje commented.

"What I mean is that an ordinary person wouldn't eat your meals. So I'd like to teach you some ordinary home cooking," Milia clarified.

"...If you insist. There is nothing I cannot master, after all."

"Where do you get that self-confidence from?"

The two women set to their task.

I was so shaken up, I just stood there for a while.

Rila and Roje had spoken with the kids a lot and had learned many things, so I asked the latter for a report.

The youngest child was seven years old, and the oldest twelve. There were four boys and six girls. Roje made it clear that none of them had homes or families to return to.

"I see. Perhaps we can use the Adventurers Guild's connections to find them new guardians," I posited aloud.

The farmers who often came to us with requests would undoubtedly be glad for more help. Although the work would likely be difficult, all the farmers I knew were good people, and I could rest assured the children would be in good hands.

Looking displeased, Roje explained, "When I asked them how they came to be in such an awful place, they told me that slave traders brought them there. It's likely that they were determined to be unsellable."

The children weren't outstanding in any regard. Maybe this was the fate of a lot of people in similar situations.

"Now, Milia, what is next?"

"Hmm... You're as quick a learner as ever..."

"Ha-ha. Naturally."

Roje looked dejected as she watched Rila and Milia.

"She never is like that with me... Lord Rileyla looks as though she is enjoying herself..."

I gave her a good push toward the other two women. "Miss Milia, this elf would like you to teach her as well."

"Wha—? You bastard! I never said such a thing at all—"

"Oh? That's fine. I love teaching," Milia replied, beaming.

Bashfully, Roje joined in. Once she had, I made for the Adventurers Guild.

I gave Iris my report of what had happened on the broadscale quest.

"What?! ...How did this turn into something so serious?!" Consternation was written large all over her face, and she coiled a lock of her hair around a finger. "If the aristocracy is involved, there's not much we can do... You see, nobles often have their own tacit agreements, things that they've arranged secretly... Their word is like law in some regions. Bad things can happen to outsiders who try to stick their noses where they don't belong..."

"Would you like me to take you? So you can see the slave-hunting show for yourself?" I questioned.

"Okay, look, I'm disgusted to know they're doing such inhumane things, too... It's just..." Iris trailed off, only groaning.

Slaves were fully beholden to their owners, so they couldn't utter a word of complaint or fight back. However, treating their lives like playthings was taking it too far.

Taking this matter up with Lord Bardel, the ruler of this district, would be difficult. Authority varied from one area to the next, and raising even a word against the lordship of another region could spark hostility.

"I'll report this to the headquarters. Roland, you have connections in the castle, don't you? I don't think anyone could resolve this matter unless they were *very* high up."

Iris was hinting that I should secretly consult King Randolf.

"I see. Then I'll leave the rest in your hands."

I bowed and left the branch manager's office.

Dinner was waiting for me when I returned home, and the dining room table was practically bustling.

Rila, Roje, Dey, Milia, Lina, and the children sat around it with me. Our normal table wasn't nearly spacious enough, so we were using the one from the living room. I didn't like how noisy it was, but it felt strangely "warm."

Now that I'd recovered some mana, I made the jump to the capital.

As usual, I slipped by the lackluster guards and right into the king's bedchambers.

"*Smooch, smooch, smooch.* Catrinaaaaa, *smoooch.*"

"Oh, my king, must you? Oh, I've coddled you, I have."

Things were getting steamy in bed for King Randolf and one of the beautiful women who served him.

"Hey there, King."

"NgaaAAAAAAAAAAAH?!"

"Ahhhh?! Wh-who are you?!"

"Th-that voice! Is that you, Roland?!"

The woman quickly covered her top half with a blanket as King Randolf's eyes darted around.

"Sorry for disrupting your fun. You, scram."

I jerked my chin, pointing outside. The woman looked at King Randolf for confirmation.

"*Ahem*. You may take your leave," he told her.

"I—I shall…"

After gathering up her undergarments and gaudy clothes, she scampered away.

"Come now. What is it this time? Why must you come when I'm busy?"

"Sorry for interrupting your child-making. There's a matter I need to consult you on."

"This…seems like it won't be a very pleasant conversation."

"Naturally."

I explained what had happened during the broadscale quest.

"The guild likely won't be able to intervene…," I concluded.

"You're right about that. Lina's orphanage is in Imil, the second largest city in the country. The Moisandle marquis family governs that area. They're a great house with distant relations to the Felind family."

Imil was also surrounded by many incredibly wealthy towns, possessed a large port, and was a key location for trade and commerce.

"Do you have any idea how important the earnings received from the Moisandle household are to the kingdom as a whole, Roland?"

"Please don't give me that. I didn't come here to argue politics."

"It's actually a quarter of our income. They surpass forty-seven other noble clans by a great lead. Without their backing, we wouldn't have stood a chance in the Human-Fiend War."

"So what about that?"

"I'm saying I'm sorry."

"..."

"The easy part was solving who committed the crime. But I have granted Lucas Moisandle autonomy over that region. I don't doubt the crimes you accuse him of, and I sympathize with your outrage. However, in this particular instance, it's *because* I'm the king that I can't get involved."

"Can you tell Lina that to her face?"

"I'm sorry; truly I am. There are other ways I can supply her with money."

I doubted Lina would be able to manage the funds on her own. Lucas Moisandle already controlled any financial support from the crown, and he would undoubtedly recruit a new orphanage director who agreed with whatever he said before long.

Nothing was going to change.

"Lina is trying to save the orphanage that raised her. All while unawares that a leech is sapping her lifeblood away," I stated.

"...Roland, a kingdom cannot function on ideals alone."

"Are you suggesting I turn a blind eye to what is happening in that arena?"

King Randolf went silent for a moment, but that itself was an answer. Then he suddenly declared:

"I did not hear of any of this today. And you did not speak to me about any of this."

"It seems I've misjudged you, King Randolf."

"Since you've told me nothing, I am unaware of what you may be planning to do next. Even if, say, a certain marquis was to be assassinated."

"I apologize for interrupting your evening," I told him, then left through the window.

Come nighttime, Lina was unable to sleep. From under my blanket, she whispered, "Was I abandoned...? They found out I could use lots of magic, and I wanted to help my father..."

The poor girl had been saddled with all manner of titles— prodigy, genius, monster—before becoming one of Almelia's companions in the party of heroes.

"He was sooo nice to me, so it was my turn to be realllly nice to him," Lina muttered while dozing off.

The girl had only ever sought to save the place that rescued her. Even now, that wish drove her forward. Lina squeezed my sleeve as she slumbered.

I informed Rila, Roje, and Dey about the situation in the living room.

"I cannot fathom how many of my army this child sent to an early grave... However, what transpired during wartime and our present issue are separate matters," Rila remarked. Dey and Roje agreed, content to leave the past where it was.

"Lina sure has gone through a lot...," Dey said.

"I wholeheartedly agree, but that doesn't help us figure out what to do. The marquis is a distant relative of the royal family, and though he hosts an underground arena, his family contributes greatly to the kingdom and is widely respected. How can we hope to stand against them?" Roje replied.

"It will be difficult to squash that place. We'll need people and magic that will pack a punch. Those are both things I'm not good at," I added.

Rila abruptly stood as though she'd been waiting for this moment. "Then it seems my time has come!"

Roje gave her a small round of applause. "Genius, Lord Rileyla, as always."

Some things never changed.

"You can claim it's your time to shine all you want, but you don't have any mana," I stated.

"Mm-hmm. I am well aware. However, the new ritual I have contrived may very well blow the place away."

While she could no longer use spells herself, there likely wasn't a single soul in the world who could rival Rila in magical sensibilities.

A new ritual that the former demon lord herself thought up, huh?

"According to magical theory, it should not be a problem... However, I obviously cannot test it on my own."

Which meant it couldn't be employed in real combat.

"Then tell me once it's actually usable. Anyway, I'm going to have a talk with that venerable family," I declared.

I slowly pulled Lina's hand off me and picked her up, then handed her over to Rila.

"Knave... Iris told you that the guild cannot get involved, did she not?"

"This isn't work. It's...a favor for a friend."

There was nothing wrong with removing a parasite that was living off Lina's purity. Pest extermination was always been something I've been good at.

"If anything happens, you might be fired, Master Roland...," Dey objected, seeming lonesome.

Roje added, "I am not worried for your sake at all, but if it would cause Lord Rileyla an inconvenience..."

"Who do you think I am?"

Rila snickered. "You are a treacherous man who is particularly good at making his own achievements out to be others' successes."

"Yeah, that's right."

That was what I was—a shadowy and harsh man.

"I'll be back for work."

The three women stared at me as though they had more to say, but I brushed off their gazes and departed.

◆

I used a Gate to return to the underground arena through the emergency exit and headed to the true entrance. There were no guards stationed by the access, as it was meant to be a secret way out, and I had no trouble moving through the place.

Of course, there was a rather burly soldier guarding the standard egress, but I knocked him out and finally got outside.

The main entrance was connected to a hill that overlooked the western area's largest city—Imil. That explained why the passage was so long. The sprawling settlement was divvied up by ramparts into large wards that rivaled the royal capital's own. There was a port district, a residential district, a business district, and in the center of it all, a venerated castle on top of a small knoll.

Imil hadn't been dubbed Felind's second largest city for nothing.

Though it was late into the night, I could still see many lights coming from the business district. Hoping to gather some information, I made my way to a boisterous tavern there, took a seat at the counter, and ordered some food.

Places like this were the standard for intel hunting. Alcohol could get anyone to talk so long as you played the part of an interested listener. Whether they were on an equal footing, or if one was higher than the other, or even if they had an entirely different relationship...

"I'm looking for a capable man with a large build. He's got a particular manner of speaking. I believe his name is Mr. Paska or some such," I said to the barkeep, who seemed to know who I was describing. I had found my target sooner than anticipated.

"Yes. I believe you must mean Hamlainen. Paska Hamlainen."

"Do you know him?"

The barkeep's expression clouded over, and he winced. "He's famous hereabouts. Though, I'd say he leans more toward infamy. He's the leader of the Order of Chivalry that supervises Imil."

"Oh? I see."

The barkeep looked around as though he was checking for prying eyes, then he brought his face close to mine and whispered, "He seems to be pretty close to his lordship. So he 'supervises' in whatever manner he sees fit, if you catch my drift. We never had these issues in the old days, yet ever since the change of power, Hamlainen has been taking a protection fee..."

If someone refused to pay up, Paska confiscated their property and threw them in jail.

A loud cackle sounded across the room, and the barkeep scowled and pulled away.

The man himself had arrived with six—no, seven—men in tow.

"Very busy today, I see. Very, very. That must mean business is going well."

While he spoke and acted differently compared to when I had last seen him, I knew it was Paska Hamlainen.

"Yes... Thanks to you..." The barkeep greeted Paska with a forced smile and a nod.

Moments ago, this establishment had been quite lively, yet now it was as silent as the grave. Everyone looked wary, eyeing Paska and his men to see if they were in good spirits or not. Some patrons even snuck away.

I listened in on Paska's conversation with his gang from the counter.

"Really? You think so, Captain?" one of Paska's men asked in a throaty voice.

Nodding, Paska replied, "Yes, I think I'll be made an aristocrat before long."

"They're that grateful for all your doing, eh?"

"Well, something like that."

There was no limit to the number of nobles. Anyone could buy a title. If one was fortunate enough to have an aristocratic friend, you could pay them for a recommendation, too. Capital and connections were all it took to climb the social ladder.

"I see..."

Now I understood why he'd dragged Lina into this.

"You'll get to sleep with all the women you want, and you won't have to work a day in your life again. I'm jealous already," one of Paska's henchmen remarked.

"Well, when the time comes, I'll take you up as Hamlainen knights."

"I'd be much obliged, sir."

Paska's crew wasn't shy about sucking up to him.

"Here's the payment for the bill." Paska tossed some money on the table.

It was made up entirely of change, and nowhere near enough to cover food and drinks for all his men.

With a gloomy expression, the barkeep bowed his head. "...Thank you very much."

"I'll be back later," Paska declared before he and his entourage left.

"How much was that, boss? It didn't seem like enough to cover all of us?"

"You think so? I didn't hear any complaints. It must have sufficed."

"Looks like you can get away with near anything. Ha-ha-ha."

The ruffians' inane laughter echoed into the night.

"How long will this keep up, I wonder...?" the barkeep muttered as he gathered the paltry sum.

I placed a little more than I should have on the table. "It's all right. I don't need any change."

Standing, I hurried after the goons.

There was something I wanted to hear directly from Paska. Since his men would only get in the way, I sneakily nabbed each one from behind, knocking them out and leaving them in alleys.

"Oy, any of you listening?" Paska yelled behind him, not realizing that his entourage had dried up.

When he did turn around, his eyes met with only mine.

"...Who the hell are you?"

"You're going to tell me what I want to know about the director of the orphanage," I stated.

"Huh? What's your problem...? Did that kid say something to you?"

"Answer me. There was an orphanage director who went to appeal to the lordship for money once the budget dried up. Where is he? I heard he was jailed. That wasn't done fairly, was it?"

Paska scratched his head, looking irked. Then he started to chuckle.

"Yeah, you got that right. Ha-ha-ha-ha." He slapped his forehead as if he could not think of anything more amusing. "I think there was a grimy old man who came by trying to beg for money. *'The children are going hungry.'* The broke beggar was weeping! Ha-ha-ha!"

"...What happened to him?"

Paska stifled his chuckles as a nasty smile formed over his face, and he shouted in delight:

"Guy's already looong dead!"

"I see... That's too bad," I replied.

In order to hold back the rage that was simmering within me, I took a deep breath and closed my eyes. I'd hoped to rescue the man Lina saw as her father. This was truly unfortunate.

"What else were we going to do? The prisons are full of criminals. That's what the Order of Chivalry's job is; it's how we keep this place safe. Then we got this stupid little kid coming by asking where her daddy was."

"...You mean Lina?"

"How's that little scamp the same genius mage from the party of heroes? She hasn't got a siiingle clue how the world works. She's just a little tyke. Her dad or whatever was already long gone by the time she stopped by."

"That's enough. I get it. Stop talking."

This guy truly believed he would become an aristocrat through the money he'd leeched off Lina?

Paska continued, as though he were telling a joke, "That's when I had this spectacular idea, see? I told her if she wanted to save her father, she'd need money. And get this—I said I knew this great place where she could really rake it in. That kid totally bought it—all for a guy who's not even alive!"

"I won't have you continuing to insult my friend any further," I said.

"Your friend? Heh, what are you gonna do? I'm head of the Order of Chivalry in Imil."

"Don't worry. There are plenty of people who could replace you."

I didn't even need to use my skill on this drunk lout.

Paska reached for the sword at his hip. At the same time, I moved in, grabbed his spare blade, and stabbed it through his boot.

"Gaaaaaaah?! M-my foot! My sword!" Paska was making a racket.

"...Don't think your death will be an easy one."

Gritting his teeth, Paska tried to bring his weapon down on me.

"Aghhhhhh!"

"Are you truly any different from a kid who doesn't know the way of the world?"

I dodged and dropped low while holding myself up by my hands, then I lodged my foot in Paska's mouth.

"Gfwoh?!"

"Enjoy the taste of my shoe, do you?"

Once I'd knocked the man down, I took his sword and used it to pin his hand to the ground.

"Aaaah! Aaaaaah?!"

I stabbed his other palm through with a fork I had taken from the tavern earlier. I didn't need him tugging his arms free, so I made sure to really drive the fork in for good measure.

"Ow, ouch, owie, owwwiiiiie…" Paska sobbed as he writhed. "Someone help…hewp… Someooone… I can't move… It hurts…"

People had started to gather to watch, but none of them said anything.

Then one person threw a rock at the man pinned to the ground and shouted, "D-die you bastard!"

"Yeah, hurry up and croak!"

"No one's gonna help you!"

I took a knife from someone who tried to rush forward to attack Paska. The onlookers were just normal passersby; I couldn't have them getting involved.

I held the small blade I had confiscated in a backhand grip and began to slice through Paska's arteries one at a time.

"Very popular, I see. I'll let you die with filth all over your face. You're an embarrassment to the knights."

I stared down at Paska's agonized expression with a cold look until he finally expired.

Several Order of Chivalry members were on their way, so I withdrew. Afterward, I went to the Order of Chivalry's station and sought out the most honest man I could find, then explained the situation.

Fortunately, not everyone in the Order was like Paska or his goons. As we spoke, I learned that the man was the vice captain. He'd opposed Paska's actions for a long time but had never been able to do anything about him. The vice captain also made it clear just how close the corrupt marquis and Paska were.

"It seems like I really do need to act, then…"

I headed to the castle, which was shrouded in the shadow of night.

Guards patrolled the area, but none of them seemed liable to notice me. Thus, I didn't bother to use my skill and merely crept into Lord Moisandle's estate.

Once inside, I climbed to the top of a staircase and searched for the marquis's room.

Important people often guaranteed they would have a path of emergency egress in their own homes. Based on the construction of the castle, it seemed there was an underground escape passage. Knowing that, I worked backward to suss out where Lord Moisandle would be.

Once I found a chamber that seemed to fit the bill, I headed straight in through the door.

"Who is it?"

I found a young aristocrat sitting behind a large desk, his slender, gentlemanly face illuminated by lamplight.

"Are you aware that Lina, the girl from the party of heroes, lives in the orphanage?" I questioned.

"Who are you? What are you talking about?"

"Paska told me everything. Even that you arrested the orphanage's director under false charges and killed him. I know you've been pocketing the money meant for Lina."

Lord Moisandle clucked his tongue softly.

"And who are you?"

"I am from the kingdom of Felind's special public welfare division."

I used the same fake title I had once before.

"Never heard of the place."

"That's because it's an intelligence organization that reports directly to His Majesty. An aristocrat like you wouldn't know about it. Please return the funds you embezzled. Also, please abolish that abominable underground arena."

"…Who do you think you're talking to? I am Lucas Moisandle."

"Your station does not affect my requests."

Lord Moisandle put down the pen he had been holding and said, as much to himself as to me, "You have no idea. You have no clue at all. Who do you think is keeping Felind afloat? That's me! I, the head of the Moisandle household!"

"I shall repeat this as many times as I need. I do not care who you are."

Lord Moisandle glanced outside the door.

"The knights won't be coming. Especially that one you seem to be so reliant on, Paska."

That man was little more than dog food now. I'd even left a fork, so the hounds could have a civilized sit-down meal.

I took a step closer, and Lord Moisandle clattered backward out of his chair.

"Stay away, you peasant!"

"I'm not sure where a lowlife gets off calling someone a peasant."

"That underground arena is a necessity. Especially for people with money and time to spare."

"Are you prepared to tell that to the children who die for the amusement of your bored rich people?"

"Why should I concern myself with them?! I hear that none of the nobles or merchants who come to the events resort to violence themselves. Do you know why? It's because they satiate their need for blood there! It quiets their destructive proclivities!"

Lord Moisandle was attempting to push his crimes as a necessary evil.

"Deny it all you like; you're already cornered. His Majesty doesn't agree on the necessity of such a barbaric installation."

Distress showed plain on the marquis's face.

"Wha...? What do you want from me?!"

"Return the money you misappropriated and cough up everything you spent on the arena, too."

"Wh-why?"

The building used for the underground death matches was old. However, it had clearly been refurbished to accommodate wealthy spectators.

Anxiety started to show on Lord Moisandle's once calm and collected face.

"Th-that was originally Moisandle money…! Do you under-stand the sum I bring in for the kingdom?"

"The taxes are redistributed to each of the regions. The crown is not demanding unreasonable payments that require you to go to such extremes," I replied. King Randolf had explained all that to me once.

"But we also financially supported the war effort! We Mois-andles sacrificed our own fortune, yet we received nothing in return!"

"Had we lost, you likely would have died, making your land and wealth utterly worthless."

This man really pinched his coins.

"K-keep back! Who do you think I am?!"

"I don't like people who feel the need to continuously repeat themselves."

"What's so wrong about holding a bit of amusement in my own territory?!"

"About that… I visited your establishment today. It may inter-est you to know it actually isn't within your jurisdiction. The arena just barely crosses into Lord Bardel's land."

"What…?" He foolishly let his mouth fall open. "N-nonsense! W-we created an entrance so we could enter it from our territory! So it is the Moisandle household's arena!"

"What unreasonable logic."

I kicked the desk, producing a much louder noise than I'd expected.

"Yeek?!"

"So what will you do? Will you return what you owe? Or will you go crying to King Randolf?" Moisandle had no leg to stand on now that he knew his illicit arena was in Lord Bardel's territory. "Once the truth comes out, your name will go down in history as an uncivilized bottom-feeder."

"Y-you bastard...! I failed to mention this earlier, but the Moisandle household is a distant relative of the royal family! Attacking us is as good as drawing steel against the king himself!"

Seeing that his first line of defense had crumbled, the man was trying to hide behind the Felind royal family. I was so beyond exasperated it was almost comical.

"King Randolf elected to remain ignorant of my actions tonight," I revealed.

"Y-you lie! Why would he f-forsake the Moisandle family?! Why would he cast out Lucas Moisandle?!" the marquis wailed. He almost seemed as though he was about to cry.

"He hasn't forsaken you; he's given up. You spent money meant for an orphanage on an illegal establishment and used the place for barbaric acts that would disgust anyone. It would be wise of you to prepare for the worst."

"B-but..."

Lord Moisandle backed up all the way to the wall and slumped down. With a lowered head, he pleaded, "I'll give it all back... Please, just turn a blind eye to this..."

"I'm afraid I can't. King Randolf needs to be apprised of everything. I'll need to report all of this to King Randolf."

"What...? What will happen to...?"

"You'll likely need to dismantle all your operations."

Balling his fists, Lord Moisandle cried, "You can't be serious?! There will always be a market for that kind of entertainment! No matter what you do, it won't end with me!"

Suddenly, a brilliant light illuminated the room, and everything shook. Through a window, I could see black smoke and a giant cloud of dust billowing up in the distance, even at this late hour.

"Wh-what was that?" Lord Moisandle inquired.

"It...came from the arena," I replied.

Wait...

"Wh-what happened?! I spent a fortune getting everything in that place perfect!" The marquis stood himself up and pulled binoculars from a drawer. "I-it's been blown away?!"

I seized the binoculars from him. Indeed, when I check where the subterranean arena had been, there was now only a massive crater. Some immensely powerful magic had eradicated it. I also spotted a few people sneaking away from the scene. Since the little mage was asleep, I could hazard a fair guess who was responsible.

"You can...do whatever you'd like with me..."

Evidently, Lord Moisandle had finally broken.

I made a Gate to take him directly to the capital.

I paid another visit in the middle of the night to King Randolf's bedchambers to find him alone and working on paperwork. There, I explained all that had transpired.

"...I see. So it was located in another family's dominion... Oh, but I see you haven't killed him, Roland."

"I can't slay every villain in existence. I prefer to only take out the ones I have to."

What's more, Lord Moisandle was related to the royal family. King Randolf had hinted that I could off him, but I thought it would be for the best to let the king decide his punishment.

I grabbed Lord Moisandle's hair as he hung his head and made him face me.

"Hey."

"Yeek!"

"Next time you do something, I'll end you as mercilessly as I did Paska. Remember that."

"Y-yessir..."

Fear was the most effective way to get another to change their ways.

"Roland, I'd like to thank you for your services. There's no hope in reforming the man, but he shares Felind blood, nonetheless. We can't forget that dreadful arena, either. And I must apologize for not assisting you earlier."

"That's all right," I replied. "It's almost morning."

"Would you care to join me for breakfast?" King Randolf invited, but I turned the invitation down.

"Sorry. I won't be able to make it home to work at this rate."

Plus, I needed to get back before Lina awoke.

◆

When I got to my front door, the sun had already begun to rise.

"It appears you kept good to your word. Welcome home."

Rila was there to greet me.

When I got to the living room, I found Roje and Dey waiting to hear all the details.

"One of the people leeching off of Lina is dead, and the other will receive punishment meted out by the king. That settles matters amply, I believe."

I glanced at the three, and they all nodded, seeming content.

"By the way, the arena conspicuously exploded... Any ideas as to what might have caused that?" I asked.

"Oh my, that sounds terrible," Dey responded. A grin spread across her face as she shrugged.

"I-indeed... I heard a cacophonous sound... However, I had not a clue it was the underground structure... Hmm, I see." Rila couldn't look me straight in the face.

"I-it's not like any of us did it! Y-you better not get the wr-wrong idea! I'm not dead tired after having used all my mana, either!"

The elf among us was truly a terrible liar.

"Well, I have no idea who's responsible, but it was a great help. That's all I have to say about it."

"""""..."""""

The trio of women exchanged looks and slowly broke into smiles.

Lina, likely having been roused by our chat, rubbed her eyes as she made her way over.

"Roland..."

"Sorry. Looks like we woke you."

"I thought…you left again…"

The girl stumbled toward me and wrapped her arms around my waist.

"You're okay now. You don't have to work tirelessly anymore," I assured.

"I'm not okay. I'm not okay unless you're with me, Roland…"

She had seemingly been worried after getting up and realizing I wasn't there.

I let Lina remain latched on and took her to the bedroom, then tucked her back beneath the covers and remained at her side until she passed out. At some point, my nose caught the faint scent of oil and wheat. I ventured to the kitchen where Rila, Dey, and Roje were preparing some food.

"Milia taught us!" Rila declared, looking wholly pleased with herself. For once, it wasn't empty pride, either. Breakfast that morning was a cut above standard quality.

"To put it simply, cooking is rather like magic," Rila stated, looking smug over her epiphany.

"You never cease to impress, Lord Rileyla!"

"You see, this is mere child's play to me! Ha-ha-ha-ha! There is nothing beyond me!"

"Your homemade meal is delicious, Lord Rileyla! I would like to request more."

"We must save some for Lina," Rila chided. "Make do with what you have."

"Yes, ma'am."

Lina had only just fallen asleep, but it appeared I had to wake her up again, then I'd head to work.

After I got to the office, I told Milia about breakfast and thanked her.

"Oh, good! Still, I can't help but feel as though I've aided the enemy..."

She looked to have mixed feelings about Rila's successful cooking.

"What happened with that thing we discussed?" Iris questioned, so I gave her the summary of events.

"The arena was blown away, and the person managing it will be punished, so I think it won't be happening again," I concluded.

"R-Roland, you didn't...?"

"No. Of course, I don't have the raw strength to accomplish something like that."

Iris narrowed her eyes in obvious doubt. "Really?"

I wasn't all-powerful.

The days following the destruction of the arena passed quietly.

King Randolf gathered all the nobility and informed them of everything that had occurred in Imil.

Almelia stopped by my place and stated that, "The most requested punishment was reducing the size of his territory. However, I later heard from my father's close associates that the Moisandle household had been using their achievements and proximity to the royal family as excuses to do as they please for a while. This recent business isn't their only crime."

I had no idea when Lucas Moisandle had taken over, but according to Almelia, King Randolf hadn't been able to put an end to those earlier illicit activities, either.

"...Father said he believes it right to execute him."

"How harsh," I replied.

"But it was all just an act. If he had been intending to do that, he never would have gathered the nobles and made a proclamation like that."

"I see. This is his way of deterring others from doing the same things."

There were many who wouldn't listen even when merely told not to do anything illegal.

"Yes. He wanted to demonstrate that even someone from a venerated lineage with a territory that included a large city could not act with impunity. And as a result, a family with a blood connection to the royal family tarnished their own name and was stripped of their title."

"I'm sure it must have seemed a very harsh punishment to the aristocrats," I said.

Truthfully, it was rather lenient, but most of the nobles had thought reducing Lord Moisandle's land was the best discipline.

King Randolf had handled this very well.

Undoubtedly, he had already decided what the punishment would be from the start.

"So the Moisandles were ultimately made into an example," I remarked.

There were definitely many challenges involved with the political side of this that I wasn't aware of.

"It's so difficult being the king... You have to decide how to maneuver between power balances with the nobility that no one can actually see...," Almelia stated, sounding as though she wasn't involved in that herself. "Also, Roland, I'm going to be in charge of Lina's orphanage! As the director! I'm the director!"

"I see. Then I can rest easy."

Lina had invited the hot-blooded hero-princess to take the role, although she looked to be regretting that decision.

Imil would be entrusted to nobles that King Randolf held more confidence in.

"I'm worried...about Ally..." Lina, who sat next to me, swung her legs as she spoke.

"Why do you say that?" Almelia questioned, chagrined.

"You get mad so quick..."

"Grrr..."

"You'll have to keep a close eye on her, Lina," I responded.

"I wish it were Roland. I want to...live with you..."

Almelia had a smug expression. The sort one might wear after winning something. "Too bad; you can't get Roland. He works as a guild employee, so he's too busy."

"Uwwgh... Ally, you're so mean. I hate you..."

"Well... I wanted to live with him, too..." Almelia pouted. "How about a house share? That's what they're called, right? If you start up one of those, I could come stay with you."

"What are you talking about? You live in the fanciest home in the entire country as it is," I shot back.

Almelia slumped. "I can't believe you live with Rila, of all people..."

Incidentally, Rila was out shopping at the moment.

I'd been chaperoning Lina around, then had run into Almelia, and the three of us wound up going to my place.

"I even k-kissed you, Roland... You still won't consider me in the slightest?" the princess grumbled. Upon hearing that, Lina perked up and looked at me.

"You kwissed? With Ally?"

"It was half by accident."

"I-it wasn't! A tender kiss like that could never have been! Especially since you're always so strict! It was like a kiss from a prince, even though you're an assassin!"

"I quit that business."

"Then what are you now? A prince?!"

"You already said it—I'm a guild employee."

"See, you do get mad right away, Ally..."

"Almelia's got bigger issues than that."

"Nggggggh, this is so frustrating!"

I could hear someone snickering from the next room. It was a lady-in-waiting who had come with Almelia. The princess scowled as she glared daggers at her attendant.

"I spoke with Lord Bardel, the one who governs Lahti, about an orphanage. He seemed receptive to running one here."

Aristocrats never wanted to manage such places... His agreeing definitely hadn't been born out of good faith. It was undoubtedly a ploy to make himself more popular. The man was as dead set as ever on climbing the ranks. I had tried convincing him to rebuild Lina's orphanage in Lahti, but that proved a bridge too far. The enslaved kids who I had freed the other day would also stay at Lina's orphanage for a while.

"What an unusual aristocrat. I'm surprised he would want to manage an orphanage."

"It hasn't been long since the war. There are still a lot of misplaced children from the carnage. What do you think happens when you gather them together and give them a proper education?"

"They grow into proper adults?"

"That's right. If you leave them alone, they end up sold off as slaves, but raise them right, and they'll make for an outstanding workforce. That, in turn, would increase the town's population and bolster production," I explained.

There was no telling if the kids would actually stay in Lahti once they grew up, but when I told Lord Bardel of all the benefits, he'd eaten it right up.

I let him know it was an investment for a decade or two in the future, and he had begun the arrangements right away.

"If he's successful, it'll set an example for the other nobility to follow. Especially since the population is down due to the war and the demand for more laborers that created," I said.

"I see... It's not easy procuring more territory, after all," replied Almelia.

With fewer slaves, there would be less chance of them being abused. If the nobility seized the initiative in decreasing the number of enslaved people, societies' values would change and evolve. If Almelia were to tell King Randolf as much, he might see Lord Bardel's investment favorably.

Lina looked a little troubled as she glanced between Almelia and me.

"What are you talking about...?" she asked.

"Basically, your pure intentions got me started, and now I'm trying to get lots of people to be better."

Lina didn't appear to understand, but she gave me a vague nod.

Almelia cocked an eyebrow. "...I thought *you* started all this. Weren't you responsible for Moisandle's downfall and that huge explosion?"

"No, I didn't do anything."

"Really...?" Almelia gave me a dubious look, then stood up. "Well, fine. All right, Lina, we should get going. While I can't live there permanently, I would like to get a look at the orphanage."

Lina nodded and then turned to me as though she didn't want to leave.

"Roland..."

"You can come visit whenever you like. I won't go vanish on you."

"Okay."

I went outside to see Almelia and Lina off. However, Lina

suddenly let go of Almelia's hand and hurried back to me, looking like she had forgotten something.

"Roland."

"Is something the matter?" I asked her.

She motioned for me to come closer, then she gave me a peck on the forehead.

"Lina," Almelia called, and the little mage scurried off with clear embarrassment. "What were you doing?"

"It was nothing, princess," said the smiling lady-in-waiting who had watched. She gave me a nod before she, Almelia, and Lina got into a carriage and departed.

Lina peeked from the window. I gazed at her until she was too far away to see.

◆

Rila had recently learned how to make proper food, but she was constantly setting the table with the same meal over and over.

"Wh-what do you make of it...?"

"...It's as delicious as ever."

Perhaps it would have been more accurate to say it had *become* delicious.

Although I would eat it regardless, there was one thing I wasn't quite satisfied with.

"Of course, of course. Hee-hee."

Rila prepared the same food every day, then asked my opinion and gave the same reply. She never seemed to tire of it, and it clearly made her happy, so it was hard to voice any complaints. Repeatedly eating identical food hardly constituted a balanced diet, however.

I'd have to secretly ask Milia for advice later.

I stood, which prompted Rila to look at me quizzically.

"I thought you didn't have to work today."

"I'm going to check on Lina's orphanage. I haven't seen it for myself."

"Mm-hmm. Then I shall wish you well as you inspect it."

Rila saw me off, fidgeting all the while. Then she approached and gave me a hug and a quick kiss.

"Hmm? I feel as though I have forgotten to tell you something...," she said.

"If it slipped your mind, it must not have been worth telling me about."

Rila tilted her head to the side, still puzzled over whatever it was she'd meant to say.

"I'm headed out," I declared before using the Gate to jump to the location Lina had given me directions to.

The orphanage stood at the outskirts of a town that neighbored Imil. Supposedly, it had previously been a church.

Houses surrounded the structure, and as I approached, I heard the voices of children.

"Roland!"

Lina noticed me before anyone else and came running.

"Where's Almelia?"

"Ally said she has important business at the castle…"

I always believed Almelia had too much time on her hands, but evidently she did act like a proper princess once in a while.

"I see."

"Over here, over here," Lina excitedly insisted as she led me inside.

The orphanage was presently home to twenty kids. The oldest girl of those I had freed the other day gathered everyone together. A few were playing in an admittedly cramped garden, while others were having fun inside. They seemed to be enjoying themselves.

"What does Almelia do here?" I inquired.

"She plays with everyone."

"She's goofing around?"

If that was all she was providing, I had to wonder if things would be okay, especially with so many children. However, there had to be another person behind the scenes helping Almelia make sure that funds were being spent correctly.

"Is there anything troubling you?" I added.

"No. Not right now," Lina answered.

As long as the kids had what they needed, then it was safe to conclude the orphanage was being managed well enough.

While I was being led around, I caught sight of an elf outside the window.

"Hmm… Roje?"

What was she doing here?

"Hellooo?"

A familiar voice called from the front door.

"Visitors…" Lina didn't let go of my hand and instead tugged me after her to the entrance. "H-hello…," she timidly greeted.

A girl in an elegant dress holding the hand of an aristocrat woman stood before us. It was Maylee, the former slave who had lived with Rila and me for a while. She looked to have grown slightly.

"Roland, it's been too long," she said.

"It really has."

I had no idea what was going on, but then Maylee's mother, Leyte, explained, "We were hoping to make a call on your house today, but you weren't around, so the nice elf brought us all the way here."

This was likely what Rila had forgotten to tell me. She must have asked Roje to lead Maylee and her parent here.

I peeked outside to see Roje leaning against a wall by the gate with her arms crossed.

"Roland, didn't you come to play with me?" Lina reminded.

"I'm so sorry for our sudden drop-in," Leyte apologized.

"It's all right," I replied.

Lina kept a tight grip over my hand as she hid behind me. "Roland…came to visit us… So you can't right now…"

"How about we all play together?" Maylee suggested.

Lina shook her head. "Roland is my big brother… You can't take him…"

"I won't. Roland is going to be my prince consort, so it's okay."

"Then…it's all right…"

Apparently, the two children had reached an agreement of sorts.

Leyte smiled as she watched over them.

"Alias doesn't have other kids her age around, so I'm sure she's thrilled by the prospect."

"Hopefully they become fast friends," I stated.

Maylee was lively and cheerful while Lina was bashful and nervous. Though they had opposite personalities, that might lead to them getting along even better than expected. Lina introduced Maylee to the other children, and they all started to play happily.

I watched them with Leyte as we talked about what had happened recently.

Leyte had been queen of the Bardenhawk duchy, which was destroyed in the war. Fortunately, reconstruction was moving forward. After losing so many people to the fighting, it had been decided to abolish the royalty and instate elected representatives from among the populace to form a democratic system.

"She's ten right now, but she'll be an adult at fifteen in five years. When that happens, she might actually come to try to get you," Leyte remarked with a laugh. I couldn't tell if she was joking.

"It's an emotional time for her, so I'm sure someone else will catch her attention," I responded.

"Do you think so? I wouldn't mind someone as handsome as you myself."

That was difficult to dismiss as humor, leaving me hard-pressed for what to say. Leyte's husband, the king of Bardenhawk, was long dead. Maylee had likely been born when her mother was very young. Leyte appeared close to Iris's age, possibly in her midthirties. She wasn't much older than me.

The woman had radiant skin and was a true beauty.

When Leyte placed her hand on my thigh, I grabbed it and returned it to her lap.

"It's a great honor. When the time comes, I will consider it again."

"Ha-ha-ha. I've heard so much about you from Alias. I would have no qualms if you were to join our family. Please stop by anytime."

Roje stared at me from the window.

"Heh-heh-heh... The human doesn't know what to do when faced with the charms of a mature woman. I will report back on this to Lord Rileyla and make sure this lowers her favor toward you."

She was cooking up an awful scheme.

Lina and Maylee seemed to be hitting it off well.

Deciding it would be best not to interrupt them, I quietly excused myself from the orphanage.

"Hey, where are you going?" Roje called out to stop me.

"I was invited to lunch. I'll leave taking the two of them back to the house to you."

"You needn't tell me that. Lord Rileyla entrusted them to me."

"Excellent. I've nothing to worry about, then."

I used the Gate Roje had apparently made to set up a path to the capital and jumped there.

Once in the castle, I went in search of King Randolf, who had invited me.

He wasn't in his bedroom, where I usually found him. According to his servants, he was in the dining room. I made my way there and saw that he was in the company of two others.

King Randolf let out a grand laugh. "You're late, Roland."

"That's because you never told me where you would be," I replied.

Next to him was Tallow Paulo. The guild master's angular face was unshaven, as it regularly was.

"There you are, Roland. Seems you've been getting up to some interesting antics. I suppose that's rather commonplace for you, though!"

"Your voice is too loud, although that's rather commonplace for *you*."

"What are you talking about? It's my only redeeming quality."

"Yeah, yeah," I answered, to which Tallow let out a boisterous laugh.

"I was told there would be one more person, but I had no idea it would be you," stated the third man. It was Frank Lanperd, the head of the imperial knights. Born into poverty, he'd risen to the top with nothing but a spear. He was an officer in the army and one of the people besides my master who had taught me the art of weapon fighting.

His goatee, which didn't suit his slender face, was one of his defining characteristics.

Frank had only instructed on how to wield spears, but he was unsurpassed with them. If we fought head-on with nothing but spears, I would lose. Should that ever come to pass, however, the key would be not to attack him from the front.

"Roland, it's been a while. I heard you had gone missing, so I was convinced you had died. Then Tallow informed me that you were still kicking."

Frank and I shook hands.

"Many things have happened, but I've managed to endure."

I sat down and had a lunch with the trio of familiar faces. Though they mostly spoke of the kingdom and other matters that didn't concern me, they did occasionally ask for my opinion.

"So you were the one who proposed opening more orphanages, is that right, Roland?" Frank stroked his short goatee as he raised an eyebrow and asked.

"Yes. For the reasons I explained earlier."

Frank cast me a displeased look. "And you're leaving the king to do your dirty work."

"Roland is the type to just find the hunting grounds for you and tell you to learn to fish," Tallow remarked with his mouth still full of food.

"What else would you expect from a simple guild worker?" I asked.

""A normal guild worker wouldn't go to all this trouble,"" Frank and Tallow said in unison.

"The kingdom is issuing funds and managing the orphanage on the outskirts of Imil as a test. If that goes well, we'll establish one in every region. Children have infinite potential. They could be bakers, adventurers, cobblers, or even farmers," King Randolf explained. It seemed that my earlier discussions with him on that matter had helped him comprehend the importance of investing in the future generation.

"Why? Why can't I go in?" I heard a voice outside the dining hall that sounded a lot like Almelia's.

"It is a four-person luncheon, Lady Almelia."

"Four to five is hardly a difference! What's wrong with me joining? I know Roland. He'll leave without even saying good-bye, so just give me a little—"

"Looks like we've got an agitator," Frank joked.

"Her Highness has taken quite a liking to Roland. She's rather like a chick who believed him her parent. Did you know? She never left his side during the great war," Tallow said, laughing again.

"Must she really ruin a nice lunch meeting?" King Randolf asked, seeming exasperated as he sighed.

I left my seat to quiet the troublesome princess.

"Hey, Almelia."

I opened the door just as Almelia had tried to pull it open, knocking her over. Fortunately, I reacted swiftly and caught her by the shoulders.

"R-Roland...?!"

Perhaps because our faces were so close, Almelia's face reddened.

"We'll have tea in your room later. Just wait for me."

"O-okay..."

I pulled the princess to her feet, and she stood there looking dazed.

"M-my heart... Just now, I felt a bittersweet pang..."

"Lady Almelia, that's what you call falling in love."

"Wh-what?"

"I'm afraid I cannot be the one to tell you more about it."

I closed the door and turned around to see Frank and Tallow grinning at me.

"Roland, I'm sorry for the trouble," King Randolf apologized with genuine sincerity.

"It's fine. I don't mind. It's my day off, after all."

After that, we chatted about unimportant topics and finished up our lunch. Once the meal was concluded, I met with Almelia for tea.

Surprisingly, she had little to say. Maybe it had something to do with that bittersweet pang from earlier.

"Almelia, I'm counting on you with the orphanage," I stated, then I headed out of the castle and back home.

Maylee was there, so the place was quite lively. Lina had joined her, and I could hear her delighted shouts echoing through the house. The whole situation filled me with a relief I didn't quite know how to describe. It felt a bit like warmth, but also something else.

"Welcome back," Rila greeted.

"Yes, thank you. I think the thing you forgot was mentioning that Maylee was coming to visit," I replied.

"Uh... It, er, was a surprise!"

I laughed off the excuse. "Sure."

"Oh, I nearly forgot." *Smooch.* Rila planted a kiss on my fore-head, then promptly giggled bashfully. "It seems we shall have an enjoyable dinner today," she added.

"You're right about that."

My rather busy day off was far from over.

"Uh, this is the place, I guess?" muttered the man. He was stand-ing before a house that sat deep in the mountains, and he held up an envelope while searching for a mailbox.

"..."

There were no other residences around, thus this had to be the location.

The letter was light, and while the man was ignorant of its contents, that hadn't stopped him from wondering. After all, he didn't know who the sender or recipient were.

All it would take to find out was opening the envelope and reading its contents. However, the man recalled the sizable one-way delivery fee he was promised and tamped down his curi-osity. As a person living hand-to-mouth in a settlement at the base of the peaks, he had no business snooping on others' messages if he wasn't prepared for what he might find.

"Please deliver this to the house deepest in the mountains."

Just as the recipient was an enigma, so, too, had been the man who'd tasked him with the delivery.

Upon reflection, the man had been suspicious, and the work had seemed shady.

Still, the large payment had brooked no refusal.

The deliveryman could just barely make out the home's interior through its dirtied windows.

There was something like a living room inside, as well as a hearth. Clearly, someone had dwelled here at one point, but it couldn't have been recently.

"Whose house is this…?"

No one was there to answer his question.

At last, he spied a mail slot on the front door and dropped the envelope inside it. Then there came a rustle from inside the shabby building.

"A-all right, looks like that does it."

He peeked in from the small opening of the mail slot and saw that the living room was deserted and covered in dust.

Would someone stop by here eventually? Perhaps someone else like him would come to get the envelope and take it to another location.

"I shouldn't think about it. Time to go home. This place is creepy."

The man shivered as he hurried to put the house behind him.

Routing a letter through multiple people was one method of delivering a request.

This was the house of the man who had once assassinated the demon lord. He and the woman who'd raised him had lived here long ago.

None needed to know that the contents of the missive detailed a target for assassination, save the sender.

Afterword

Hello, everyone. I'm Kennoji.

Like the last volume, this book features a story involving members of the party of heroes. I plan to have the other two, who haven't shown up much yet, make appearances in the future.

Personally, I really like having the adventurer Neal and the senior guild worker Maurey play supporting roles. There were a few hints to Roland's past in this installment, but in the next novel, I plan on going deeper into the matter as I build things into a bigger narrative. I hope you'll read it and enjoy.

The first volume of the manga version came out at the same time as this book! Fuh Araki drew the characters in such a charming way, so I hope that those of you who haven't read it yet will consider doing so!

Thank you so very much for sticking with me all the way to the third volume. Things will get even more entertaining as the series continues. Please look forward to it.

Kennoji